THE Beast OF THE FAE COURT

FROM USA TODAY BESTSELLING AUTHOR
ERIN BEDFORD

Also by Erin Bedford

The Underground Series
Chasing Rabbits
Chasing Cats
Chasing Princes
Chasing Shadows
Chasing Hearts
The Crimes of Alice

The Mary Wiles Chronicles
Marked by Hell
Bound by Hell
Deceived by Hell
Tempted by Hell

Starcrossed Dragons
Riding Lightning
Grinding Frost
Swallowing Fire
Pounding Earth

The Crimson Fold
Until Midnight
Until Dawn
Until Sunset

Curse of the Fairy Tales
Rapunzel Untamed

Her Angels
Heaven's Embrace
Heaven's A Beach
Heaven's Most Wanted

House of Durand
Indebted to the Vampires
Wanted by the Vampires
Protected by the Vampires

Academy of Witches
Witching On A Star
As You Witch
Witch You Were Here
Just Witch It

Granting Her Wish
Vampire CEO

This one is dedicated to my husband. My favorite asshole in all the land. I wouldn't want to irritate anyone else but you.

THE  *Beast* OF THE FAE COURT

FROM USA TODAY BESTSELLING AUTHOR

ERIN BEDFORD

Chapter 1

Balefire

WHY DID THE HUMANS love springtime so much? The birds were singing. Irritating. The flowers were blooming. Which meant I kept sneezing. One would think any sane rational person would want to stay inside where there weren't people everywhere. That's what I normally did.

Except today.

Today was the annual festival of choosing. Humans from all over the Fae Court of Spring would be competing in events to earn a place in the palace. My home. Not as part of the royal court because that would be ridiculous. A human at court? I'd rather dive headfirst into a basilisk's mouth. No, these humans were scrambling all over themselves to serve me. Balefire, the King of the Spring Court.

I took over for my father, King Wyrn, who had retired a few weeks ago. Which was the only way I was ever going to be king. Fae didn't die. Not unless someone killed them. Unfortunately, that happened on more occasions that I would have liked. Some humans just couldn't be happy with their place.

My nose drew up in a grimace as my eyes scanned around the marketplace. Rotten ungrateful cretins. They scurried to and fro like little mice, but unlike real mice, the humans were stupid. They didn't know well enough to be scared of the cats watching them, waiting to pounce if they so much as came close.

"Do you really think this is wise? Flittering about outside the castle." My groomsman, Finch, interrupted my thoughts as he gripped at me for the twelfth time since we left the palace.

Finch was a man of six hundred and fifty but to humans he would only seem about thirty with his dark curly hair brushing his shoulders and piercing green eyes. Some of the fae women at court have mooned over him on more than one occasion. However, Finch took his job seriously. Some would say too seriously.

He was only half a decade older than me, but he still treated me like a child. I wouldn't had even brought him along, but he insisted. Hovering bastard. I couldn't fault him though. Finch has been with me since I was a lad. Now that I was King, he was my closest confidant and friend. Even when he was annoying me like now.

"If someone is going to be working in my home, I would like to know who they are." I narrowed my eyes at the humans running their businesses while unaware of their king only feet away from them.

Finch frowned, his forehead bunching together. "But you could have met them when they arrived, just like your father and his father before that. There was no reason to dress up like a commoner and glamour your princely features so. You are putting yourself in unnecessary danger."

I resisted the urge to roll my eyes. I was a king now. Kings should be more mature than that. At least, my father was, and I strove to be an even better king than him.

"I'm in no danger," I reminded him, shifting my stance so I didn't look as intimidating. "No one will even recognize me, and if you had changed your features as well, there would be no suspicion at all. Now, who's the one putting us at risk?"

Finch's lips twisted into a grimace. "You know I hate glamours. It makes my skin feel too tight. And it itches." He lifted and lowered his shoulders as if trying to scratch an invisible itch.

Shaking my head at him, I turned back to the market. I had no worries about being discovered. While I had kept my body's structure similar, with large broad shoulders, a slim waist, and long legs, my predominant family features, golden skin and locks paired with sky blue eyes, were missing. In their place was a mossy head of hair, dull brown eyes, and a crooked nose. My skin had lost its sheen, and my tattoos have been covered by my long-sleeved tan shirt that I made sure was buttoned to the collar. I'd have covered them with a glamour as well, but Finch's gasp of horror was too much to handle.

"You can't hide your heritage! That's blasphemy." Finch had followed it up with a clucking of his tongue. I swore he was more like a mother hen than a fae man. Sometimes I wondered why I even kept him around.

"Very well," Finch conceded with a reluctant sigh. "If we must do this, let us get it over with. How about we check out the household cleaners? The brownies have a section set up over there to test the humans' skills before selecting the best candidate for the job." He sniffed and brushed some invisible lint from his shirt. "You know how picky those brownies can be. Obsessed with cleaning as they are."

Not wanting to argue anymore, I nodded to my well-meaning servant and allowed Finch to lead me to the brownies in a nearby building. The mud-colored fae walked up and down the aisle as they looked down their cut off noses at the humans' work. They had tables of silver dishes set up on each table and the humans scrubbed and polished until their fingers were raw. I knew that even that level of work wouldn't impress a brownie. They would reluctantly choose someone simply because they must, but behind closed doors, they would complain about how inept the humans were at basic cleaning tasks.

After standing there for several minutes, I dropped my arms from where I had them crossed and turned my head toward a delicious smell. Without announcing my departure, my feet moved toward the smell out of the building and toward a stand where several humans were preparing to create pies. Half a dozen fruit and meat pies were already on display on another table and I hurried to it as my stomach rumbled.

A fae woman stood behind the wooden table, her pale curly locks twisted upon her head and her head bent over a clipboard. Reaching a hand out, I started for some kind of berry pie, but before my fingers could curl around the pan, a sharp snap hit the top of my knuckles. Holding my hand, I growled at the fae woman.

"No touching, peasant. These are for the king. Not the likes of you." Her violet eyes glared at me, and I almost laughed at the irony. "Now, go wait over there with the rest of the rabble. We are about to begin the baking contest."

"Baking contest?" I arched a brow at the humans behind her fretting over their bowls and ingredients. "I didn't know we were in need of a new baker?"

The fae woman gave me a strange look. "The king is in need of a new one. Yes. Now get. I have things to do that don't involve talking to the likes of you."

My fingers curled into fists at her words. How dare she raise her voice to me? And with such rudeness. I had half a mind to throw her in the dungeon but then Finch jogged over to me and I remembered I was supposed to be in disguise.

"There you are, your... uh I mean, Angus." Finch's eyes slid over to the fae woman and then back to me before clearing his throat. "Don't walk off like that. I thought you got swept away by one of those brownies. They're fierce when they're cleaning." He let out a little nervous chuckle as he shook his head.

The fae woman had stopped gripping at me to stare at Finch, her eyes unblinking.

"What's this?" Finch asked, turning to the table of pies. "Oh, pies. These look great."

Blinking rapidly, the fae woman opened and shut her mouth before hurrying to say, "Yes, they're for the king." She paused and a blush covered her cheeks. "You're Lord Finch, aren't you?"

Finch looked up from the pies and gave her a bright smile causing her to blush deeper. "Yes, I am. And who are you?" He reached over the table and took her hand lifting it to his mouth.

"Vignette." She giggled and dipped her head. "I'm the head baker and have been appointed to select some new girls for the palace."

"Ah, if I'd known such beauty were living right under my nose," he said slyly, "I'd have spent more time in the kitchens. Something I will be sure to remedy as soon as I return to the palace."

I lifted my eyes to the sky at Finch's cheesy line. He could be a serious uptight bastard, but he had more women in his bed in a week than I had all my life. I bumped his shoulder to remind him of why we were here, and Finch dropped her hand.

Clearing his throat, he adjusted his shirt sleeves before turning down that flirtatious smile. "My apologies. We're here to help pick the new bakers. As you know, King Balefire is extremely particular about who handles his food and wants to be sure that whoever is chosen won't try to poison him."

Vignette paled, her eyes darting from Finch to me and back. She wasn't blushing now. I had that effect on people. I might be an attractive bastard, but most of the people were too scared of me to get to know me, which I preferred. I didn't need friends. I had subjects. Then one day we would find a politically benefiting wife for me who would rule by my side. That was what my father did, and my parents were the happiest couple I'd ever seen.

"His Majesty isn't coming, is he?" Vignette's eyes moved around the market searching for my golden figure no doubt. "No one said he would be coming today. I would have worn something different if I'd known." She ran her hands over the apron covering it in flour and brushed some hair behind her ears, her hands shaking the whole time.

I winced. Maybe I could lighten up on the fear a bit.

"No, no. He's not here." Finch reassured her keeping his eyes firmly off of me. "Please do not worry yourself. We are simply here to observe in his place. King Balefire is far too busy with running the Spring Court to come down here." This time he did slid his eyes over to me the corner of his lips quirking up as he verbally poked at me.

Tired of this conversation, I leaned on the table and growled, "So, when does it start?" I gestured my free hand to the humans behind her. "Are these it? They don't look like much."

Vignette turned to contestants and frowned. "We seem to be missing one, but I can assure you they were fully vetted before they got to this stage. Only the best of each town was allowed to come here. As you can see, we already narrowed it down to only six, minus the one who will be disqualified, if they don't arrive soon." She glanced down at her clipboard and then called out. "Ericka? Is an Ericka Burner here, yet?"

No one answered, but a couple of the human women behind her giggled and whispered behind their hands. Suspicious. Then one of the human women, a redhead with too pale of skin and too many spots on her face, walked over to Vignette.

"Um, excuse me." Her voice was high pitched and made my ears hurt.

"What is it?" Vignette asked with an irritated scowl. "We are about to start. There's no time to go back for anything now."

"No, no." The redhead grinned and swayed from side to side as she giggled. "I just wanted to tell you that I don't think Ericka is coming. She was still sleeping when we left the loft." Her eyes slyly slid back to the others. "She was drinking pretty heavily last night. I don't know about her, but I would think someone who wants this important of a job to have more self-restraint the night before the competition."

Vignette scoffed. "Humans! All of you are controlled by your baser instincts. I don't know how you've survived this long." The redhead didn't seem bothered by Vignette's comments. Not that Vignette had much room to talk as an idiot could see through the ploy the other human women were playing. "Fine. Ericka is out. Let's get started."

"Perhaps give her a few more minutes," Finch offered clearly, having caught onto the game as well. Vignette frowned at Finch's suggestion, but with a flash of that dazzling smile of his, she was all eyelashes and simpering smiles.

"Alright. It wouldn't hurt to wait a few more minutes." Vignette giggled as the redhead huffed and stomped back to her friends. Vignette and

Finch flirted for a few more minutes until I was becoming nauseated just by standing near them.

I coughed loudly. Then when it still didn't dissuade them, I did it again, but this time, I also bumped Finch, almost knocking him over. I gave him a small shrug. I couldn't help that he wasn't on his guard. He should know better.

Her face turning beet red, Vignette glanced down at her watch and her eyes widened. "Oh, my is that the time? We need to get started." Her eyes glanced around the group and then sighed with exasperation. "Is this it then?"

At the same time that the redhead and her friends said, "Yes," another voice filled with panic and slightly out of breath screamed, "I'm here! I'm here!"

I turned but instead of seeing the person behind the yelling, my senses were overpowered by blueberry pie. The goopy insides covered my eyes and nose, sliding down my face to plop on my shoes.

"Oh, my god, I'm so sorry." The voice cried out and a small hand swiped at my face, pulling some of the goop out of my way. "There was a rock and then my foot found it and then it was all just bad, bad, bad."

I opened my mouth to tell the woman rambling exactly what I thought of her excuses, but the blueberry pie filling slid into my mouth. Licking my lips, I swallowed. Not bad.

"Ericka!" Vignette cried out with outrage. "Where have you been? Do you have any idea who these people are?"

"I'm sorry, Vignette," Ericka rambled, her hands stilling on my face. "My alarm didn't go off and then I couldn't find my mixing bowl. On top of that, I had to remake my pie. Someone had sat the first one on the floor where I conveniently stepped on it."

My vision was finally cleared enough to see a petite little brunette glaring over at the gaggle of other bakers. Ericka's hair was haphazardly tied on top of her head in a messy bun with what looked like a pencil shoved through it. A long line of flour covered her left cheek. Her dark lashes surrounding her almost black eyes were sprinkled with a bit of white powder, making her look more like something that should be in a pie rather than making it. She was a complete and utter mess. Not someone I'd want working in my home even if I was a pauper and not the king.

Rage and humiliation filled my chest, and I opened my mouth to tell her such, but Finch stepped in handing me a handkerchief. "Ah, you must be Ericka. We've heard great things about you."

Ericka's eyes darted from Vignette to Finch and then to me her mouth gaping open. "Uh, hi. Not to be rude, but who are you?"

"You imbecile." Vignette hissed coming around the table to grab Ericka by the arm.

"They're from the palace. Lord Finch is the personal adviser to the king."

I watched with great satisfaction for her to realize who she was talking to and waited for that horror and shame to cross her face... and waited... and waited. This little twig of a human didn't so much bat an eyelash.

"It's nice to meet you, Lord Finch and..." Her eyes landed on me and winced. "I am so sorry again about your face, Mister...?"

"Angus," Finch provided for me, his eyes locking onto the human before us. "He's my assistant." I choked on my own saliva. When Finch smacked me on the back, I glared. "Don't mind us. We'll just be watching from the sidelines. Please proceed with the contest and good luck." He winked at Vignette before ushering me to the other side of the tables where the rest of the bakers were already set up.

When we were far enough away from Vignette, I threw his arm off of me. "Why did you have to say a thing like that?"

"Think of it as payback for making me come down here in the first place. I had shows to watch that I am now missing because of you." Finch shrugged and crossed his arms, his gaze on the contestants.

If Finch wasn't my oldest friend, I'd have him executed for speaking to me in such a manner, but besides being one of my only friends, my father always said you should have an adviser that wasn't afraid to tell you the truth even when it could make you want to kill them.

Huffing a sigh, I turned my attention back to the competition. The redhead and her friend are glaring daggers at Ericka while the oblivious girl went about her prep work.

"What do you think? Any of them decent?"

Finch stroked his jaw and watched Ericka carefully. "The one who was late, the Burner woman."

"What?" I scoffed in disbelief. "She's a train wreck. Even her name tells you how good of a baker she is. Burner. Ha! I'd sooner swallow a toad."

Smirking, Finch turned his eyes to me. "You would know, you've already tasted her pie."

Glaring at him, I shook my head with a groan. "She'd die in the first week. That human has no respect for her superiors. No sense of self-preservation."

"But look at how the others glower at her. And they clearly caused her tardiness. There has to be a reason, don't you think?"

I hummed and turned my eyes back to the brunette. She cursed as a bag of sugar fell off the table and landed on her foot. She scrambled to pick up the bag and then on her way back up hit her head on the underside of the table. My lips ticked up on one side. This could be fun.

Chapter 2

Ericka

MY LIFE OFFICIALLY SUCKED. Not only was I not going to win this contest, but I already messed up big time. A pie to the face was not the kind of impression that you should leave on the fae who could make or break your chances of working in the palace.

My mom was right. I hate saying that, but it's true. I never should have entered this damn contest, but I wanted to get out of our small podunk town, and this was the only way I saw out of it. Well, it was either that or becoming a stripper, and I just didn't have the coordination for that. Besides, when human men could look at fae women, the human strippers just didn't get paid the same.

"You might as well quit You're never going to win." The redheaded she-bitch, Colette whispered snidely as she accidentally knocked my bag of sugar off the table.

Pretending to have a laser that shot out of my eyes, I aimed them on her fake face and bent down to get the bag. Colette had been all smiles and compliments the first day of this contest but then the moment she found out I was from Boggsville, she and her horde of gigglers flipped their attitude real quick.

Boggsville wasn't all bad. Yes, we lived right next to the bog but there were some great things about the town of fifteen hundred people. We had that boat tour you could take of the bog and while it did stink like the back end of a troll with diarrhea, it had some pretty interesting views. Assuming, of course, you liked to look at a bog.

Unfortunately, besides the bakery I worked at owned by my mother and father, that was all Bogsville had going for them. We were poor, and it showed. But despite the smell and the paltry entertainment, humans and fae alike would come from neighboring towns just to get a taste of my mom's famous pies and quiches, something she thankfully passed along to me.

It was her blueberry pie that had gotten me into this contest in the first place. Of course, I couldn't make anything else but pies and quiches, but they didn't know that. I figured I'd just wing it when I got the job. It couldn't be that hard, could it?

And sure, a last name like Burner kind of killed people's expectations of what we could do, but really, I was the only one who couldn't cook more than a few things. Thankfully, that was all most of our customers ever asked for, so I didn't have to worry too much about expanding my skills. I just had to finish this last level of the contest and then I would be set for life. If my mishap at the beginning didn't already screw me over.

My eyes darted from the crust I was preparing to make to the two fae men standing nearby. The one with dark curly hair and pretty blue eyes watched us work with a surveying kind of stare as if he were calculating the odds against each of us. I wouldn't have bet on me, and I didn't expect anyone else to.

"Look at them." Colette's head minion, Janey, giggled. "I wouldn't kick them out of bed for leaving crumbs."

Colette giggled along with her. "I'd let them eat the crumbs off of me! If you know what I mean."

I rolled my eyes and began to crack my eggs and mix it with the milk. I was going to make my mom's famous ham and cheese quiche. It's always a hit and since the others were making more pies and other sugary creations, I figured I'd be a breath of salty comfort food goodness.

We each had a small portable oven on our tables, just big enough for a pie dish. I just hoped the temperature would work the same way as the oven back home. I'd suck to get down to the end and have it over or undercooked.

"Much like my love life," I muttered to myself.

"What was that?" Brei, one of the only nice ones, asked me from my other side. She was in the middle of making something with chocolate custard, but she was putting in too much sugar and was going to ruin the whole thing.

Clearing my throat, I nodded toward her bowl. "You're putting in too much sugar. The custard won't smooth, and you'll end up with a sand-in-your-mouth texture."

"Really?" Brei looked from me to her bowl and frowned. "I think you're right." She sighed. "Damn. Now I have to start over."

"No, you don't." I stopped mixing my bowl and stepped over to her table. "Just double your recipe then you won't waste any of it. Just be sure not to put too much sugar in this time." I smiled at her.

"Thanks so much, Ericka. You're a lifesaver!" Brei wrapped her arms around me and squeezed tight. I patted her on the back awkwardly before huffing a laugh as she thankfully released me. Holding me at shoulder length, she beamed down at me. "I don't care what those other stuck of women say, you're not bog sludge."

I laughed and gave her a tight smile, trying my best not to look at the other women, who were listening far too closely to our conversation. "Uh, thanks. And don't worry about it. It happens to all of us."

"One hour left!" Vignette called out.

Brei jumped in front of me, her eyes going wide. "Oh, no! I better get a move on. Thanks again, Ericka."

I shook my head and smiled despite myself. Turning back to my table, I lifted my hands to my hair and resecured my bun. Raising my eyes from my table, they locked onto the dark eyes of Angus. My hands froze in place at the disturbing expression on his face. It was a mixture of annoyance and surprise. For a moment, I wondered if he had overheard Brei and my conversation but then shrugged. No way, he was too far away. He was probably still pissed that I put a pie in his face. Hopefully, he got a taste of it. I make some damn good pie, if I say so myself.

Smirking to myself, I went back to working on my quiche. Some people used pie crust for their quiches but not me. My mother always said that the key to a great quiche was the crust. A pie crust was too thick and dry for a quiche. You had to make sure that the crust didn't overpower the contents of the dish.

As I worked, I hummed to myself. It was the only way to get myself into the zone and not think about people watching me or in this case talking behind my back. Usually, I would belt out to some pop song or another on the radio or more often than not talk to myself while cooking. But that would make me look like a crazy person - well crazier than they already thought I was. Which was why the humming was so important.

If I didn't hum, I was going to talk and then I would ramble. With the eyes and ears of so many on me, I wasn't taking the chance. There was already only a slim chance of winning since I'd already bungled up my entrance. I was lucky Vignette hadn't docked me for my pie going into Angus's face and not on the table for the king.

The king. I let a shudder go through me. I hadn't met the man myself or his father, but I'd heard that King Balefire had a temper worthy of his name, and he let it loose on any and everyone who got on his bad side. I just hoped he was easy to please and wouldn't be by the kitchens... ever.

There had been a lot of gossip about him already and that was just what was going around the contestants. Half of them were freaked out while the other half was hoping to get invited into his bed. Apparently, he was dreamy in that 'caveman throw you over his shoulder' kind of way.

Not my type.

I want a guy who would respect me and my limited cooking abilities. A man who would romance me and tell me how lucky he was to find a woman like me. I didn't really care about how he looked or even if he was human or fae. I wasn't speciest. Well, I take that back. Maybe not a troll. Or a Bogart. Those things just freaked me out.

As I finished laying out the crust on my pan, another shudder went through me, which was then a snort that didn't come from me. My head jerked up and my eyes narrowed on Angus, who was still watching me with an intensity that caused me to squirm. What was that guy's problem?

Angus leaned his bulky frame over to say something to Lord Finch. The lord gave Angus a disapproving frown before shaking his head. Angus smirked in my direction and I knew for sure they were talking about me.

Doomed. That's what I was, completely and utterly doomed. I might as well quit right here and now. There was no way in hell I was going to get chosen now.

I slumped at my station, my hands half-heartedly pushing the crust into place. A giggle from Colette and her group and my back straightened. That was it. I wasn't going to be beaten down by some prissy stuck up snobs just because they come from a better town than mine. Nor was I going to let some royal adviser with a stick up his ass keep me from putting my all into this contest. I came here for a reason. To win. And damn it all, I was going to.

With a renewed vigor, I shoved the crust a bit more forcefully into the pan and then poured in the filling. A mixture of ham, a couple of types of cheeses, and some green peppers. Throw in a dash of salt and pepper, some more milk and eggs and you had the recipe for deliciousness.

Shoving the pan into the preheated portable oven on my table, I let out a sigh of relief when Vignette called out, "Forty-five minutes left!"

It only took about forty minutes to cook my quiche, so I'd barely made it. Now, I had to cross my fingers, toes, and all my hairs that the time would be similar to back home. I didn't want everyone to believe my namesake on this most important day. It was bad enough when I was in school, but as an adult, being called Burner the Baker wasn't all it was cracked up to be.

"What is that awful smell?" Colette cried out overdramatically, waving a hand in front of her nose before shooting a glare in my direction. "What kind of pie are you making? Bog stench?"

Crossing my arms over my chest, I turned to Colette. "Yep, I got it from your toilet bowl. Do you want a taste?"

To my delight, Colette's face colored an eggplant purple as she tried to restrain herself from attacking me right then and there. I was sure if the advisers from the palace hadn't been there then she would be on my back yanking my hair out like any cliché girl fight. I half hoped she would. My right hand was itched to punch her right in her fake nose.

"I'm curious as well, what are you making?" A dark shadow covered my station and I abruptly twisted back around to face Angus. Lord Finch stood a few feet behind him a bemused expression on his face.

Clearing my throat, I dropped my arms and met his gaze. Such intensity from such a big man. If I was a lesser woman, I'd be a puddle on the floor. However, my insides were made of spam and fondant, not butter. Okay, that's a gross combination that I was never ever going to think about again. Clearing my throat again, I gestured to the cooking pan that certainly did not smell like a bog. It smelled exactly how it should smell, savory and mouth-watering.

"It's a quiche."

"A quiche?" Angus lifted a brow. "Why would you make a quiche at a baking contest?"

I narrowed my eyes on the fae man. Did he not know anything about baking? "A quiche is an item you bake..." I pointed a finger at the oven with some attitude. "... in the oven. It's not against the rules."

Angus's lips twitched at the sides. "I didn't say it was, but did you ever think that maybe the king doesn't like quiches? Have you ever thought of that?"

I was flabbergasted. I'd never thought of that. That was half of my baking skills. My fingers twisted into my apron and I tried not to panic. Then my eyes landed on the way Angus's eyes sparkled and a dimple appeared on one side of his face.

Seeing red, I grabbed a handful of flour and threw it at him. Immediately afterward, I gasped and scrambled to find a rag for him. "Oh, my god. I'm sorry. Here let me help you."

Colette and her gang laughed and jeered behind my back just as the bell dinged on my oven. I struggled between glaring over at them, helping Angus who was wiping flour from his eyes, and needing to get my quiche out. I couldn't let it burn...so I did the only rational thing I could in that instance. "Here," I tossed the rag at him and turned to my oven. Shoving my hand into an oven mitt, I pulled my quiche out.

Sitting it on the cooling tray, I sighed. It was perfect. The crust was just the right color of golden brown and the cheese inside had melted just the way I liked it. My relief was short-lived as a low growl came from the fae man in front of me.

Swallowing thickly, I shifted my eyes back to Angus.

His jaw clenched and his hands gripped the rag I'd thrown at him, his face still mostly covered in flour. I opened my mouth to stutter out another apology and to maybe ream him some more about teasing me when his skin began to shimmer. My tongue grew three sizes too big for my mouth when the fae man in front of me transformed.

Angus's brown hair lightened until it matched the sun. His eyes paled to a blue so light it would put the sky to shame. The dusty color of his skin took on a golden tint that almost glowed. His clothing stayed the same. but beneath the shirt, tattoos flickered with magical light, outlining the swirls and glyphs of the royal family.

A horrified gasp sounded behind me and I was shoved to the side by Vignette. A sharp pain ratcheted through my side as I hit the corner of the table next to me. My hands shot out to steady myself. I didn't have the energy to be mad at Vignette who was practically licking the dirt off of King Balefire's boots. My gaze drifted to the king himself and I suddenly realized what all the women were talking about before. He really was a beast of a man.

His long golden hair flowed down to his shoulders that was just a shade lighter than his skin. His chiseled jaw was smooth the way most fae men left their faces but was tightened into a hardened edge, that no doubt had everything to do with me. A straight nose that sat between those large blue eyes. In another setting those eyes would be beautiful but right now as they glared down at us, they were terrifying. He didn't need a crown on his head to say he was king. It radiated through and around him. My knees wobbled beneath me and I gripped the table next to me to keep myself standing.

"Now you're in for it, bog trash," Colette whispered venomously behind my back. "It was nice knowing you."

"Silence," King Balefire growled, and Vignette clamped her mouth shut with a whimper. His eyes moved from the fae woman to me. "Miss Burner, is it?"

Shoving down the quiver inside of me that I couldn't figure out if it was fear or utter humiliation. I was going for the latter. He was just a man after all. A large all-powerful man that could squash me like a bug but no matter. I'd been looked down on my whole life now shouldn't be any different. I had already resigned that I wasn't going to win today so I might as well go out with a bang!

Lifting my chin, I stared him in the eye. "That's me. And I guess that means you're not Angus?"

"No," he clipped.

I sniffed, apparently having a death wish because the word vomit just came spilling out. "Too bad. He was better looking."

A collective gasp made my throat tighten as I prepared to be punished for my words. Even Lord Finch seemed a bit worried as he moved closer to the king, but King Balefire didn't rain down fiery damnation on me like I thought he would. All he did was... smirk. In some ways, that was far worse than if he had smote me right then and there.

Leaning forward, King Balefire placed his hands on the front of my table and jerked his head toward my quiche. "Let's taste this quiche you are so sure I will like."

Vignette threw a pitying look in my direction before hurrying out of the way.

Darting at look around me at the eyes all pointed in my direction, I slowly walked toward my table. My head held high, I went about cutting him a piece of my quiche. To my satisfaction, the insides were just moist enough to melt in your mouth but not so much that it wasn't done. I grabbed a fork and held the plate up to him, smugness filling my chest and I knew the others probably thought I was insane for the grin on my face.

With a daring glower, King Balefire took the plate from me and cut into it. Without looking away from my gaze, he shoved it into his mouth and chewed. I wasn't even sure he had time to actually taste it before he swallowed and announced. "I choose her. The rest of you can leave."

A cry of outrage and dismay filled the area, but Vignette quickly rushed around the tables. "You heard His Majesty. Ericka Burner is the winner. Now congratulate her on a job well done." I couldn't see her face but from the tone of Vignette's voice she might as well have said, "And may the gods have mercy on your soul."

Chapter 3

Balefire

THE SHOCK OF HORROR on everyone's faces but Ericka Burner's pissed me off. What the hell was wrong with this human? Was she dropped on her head as a child? Perhaps she inhaled too many fumes from all the baking. Regardless, the defiant glint in her eyes only made me want to hire her even more.

I stabbed the fork into the piece of quiche on my plate and scooped it up into my mouth. Damn, that was good.

"What are you waiting for?" I growled as I chewed, jerking my chin in her direction. "Get your things and let's go."

The human should have hopped to it, grabbing her things with fearful glances my way. But no, she moved at a glacial pace as she gathered her things, taking her time to clean down her area and handing things back to Vignette. Then she had to say goodbye to every single girl there, even the ones who were being mean to her.

I shook my head and snickered. Humans. I would never understand them.

We fae were upfront about our feelings. We had to be. It was impossible for us to lie. We could bend the truth, of course, but we couldn't outright lie. Like the person I was trying to be, my first name wasn't Angus, but my middle name was, so technically, it wasn't a lie.

Little truths were how we lived. It was hard being fae around a world filled with humans who could lie to your face without consequence. That was but one of the many reasons we had to keep them in their place with just a hint of fear in their hearts.

"Are you sure this is a good idea?" Finch asked, taking me by the elbow and lowering his voice so the humans couldn't hear him but loud enough that my superior hearing could still pick up his words. "You can't hire her out of spite."

"Of course, I can. She needs to be taught a lesson, and I need something to do with my spare time." I shoved another bite into my mouth, chewed it up, and swallowed before going for another bite. Finding my plate empty, I frowned. Turning to the table, I grabbed the whole pan of quiche and discarded my plate. "Besides, I don't trust any of those conniving harpies in my home. Do you?"

I jerked my head toward the whispering and glaring human women who had done everything they could to make sure Ericka didn't win. Joke's on them. A side benefit to my little plan.

Finch eyeballed the humans before sighing. "Very well, you are the king and ultimately it is your decision, but I am telling you I am against this. So, when it all blows up in your face -"

"I know, I know. You get to say, 'I told you so,' and I'll just ignore you as always." I smirked and then handed him the empty pan of quiche. Man, that stuff goes quickly. "I'm going to go wait in the carriage, you wait for the human."

"Ericka," he said to my back as I walked away. "Her name is Ericka. You should remember it if you are going to torture the poor woman."

I waved a hand over my shoulder with a smile that I smothered as soon as the villagers realized who I was. With a scowl on my face, I stomped through the market, not talking to anyone and glowering at any who might dare step in my direction. Once I finally reached the carriage, I collapsed inside with a sigh.

It was exhausting being king. One thing my father had taught me was that, if the people didn't fear you and instead loved you, you were only a step away from anarchy. So, I did my best to be loathsome and grumpy, but I made sure they knew I treated everyone that way so they wouldn't take it personally. I was never completely cruel. I was hard but fair. At least, I strove to be.

Finding the right balance between the two was difficult. There was only so far you can go before you were seen as a tyrant, but if you were too easy on them, the citizens and other courts would think I was too soft. Then I would have revolts and declarations of war, and those were always so time-consuming. I was in the prime of my life, I didn't have time for all that.

Shifting in my seat, I glanced out the window wondering how long the human planned on making me wait. I had things to do, and none of them included sitting in a carriage on the side of the road wasting my time where anyone could just come up to me. Not that they would, but still someone might be stupid enough to approach.

My eyes drifted over the streets of the capital, mainly searching for Finch and the human woman. I refused to call her by her name. She wouldn't last that long. Not if I had anything to say about it.

The capital city, Bloomsdale, such a stupid name, but to my pride, it was cleaner than most of the other towns I'd toured in my court. Many of them didn't care enough about keeping trash off the streets or sewage where it belonged. One would think that the fae didn't take pride in their own homes, but really, it was the humans that caused the lack of cleanliness.

I often wondered why we ever let them into the fae world in the first place. It wasn't as though we were lacking for population. We had an abundance of people, and we didn't lack for anything the human world had, though electricity was a nice one. I could read by firelight just as easily as a lamp. The things we put up with for such luxuries.

There were a few other human inventions we had brought into our world, indoor plumbing being one and television another. I was thankful most days that we had put our foot down when it came to motor vehicles. They were unnecessary in most courts with the short distance between the towns and the vast majority of the fae being able to fly or teleport. Cars brought a lot of pollution to the world, something we fae did not need. On top of the fact that a lot of them were full of iron, anathema to my kind, and besides, we didn't have the resources to keep them fueled in the first place. While carriages were a bumpier ride than a motor vehicle, horses were far cleaner than the smoke that came pouring out of the former.

"Ugh," a low groan of disgust drew my eyes away from the road to the side of the carriage. The human stood there with her arms full of bags and an utter look of dismay at my carriage.

Ignoring her disapproval, my shoulders bunched up as I asked, "Where is Finch? What have you done to him?"

The human's eyes drifted from the side of the carriage to meet my eyes. Black orbs met my blue ones, and her thin brow lifted up as she glared at me with no fear. "Finch? Who's that?"

With an incredulous look, I growled through clenched teeth. "My adviser. He was just with you. Where is he?"

Blinking her eyes big and innocently at me, the human then asked, "You mean the hot guy flirting with Vignette?"

Irritation filled my chest at her description of Finch as the 'hot guy.' Already my adviser had more of her attention than me. I'd have to fix that.

I shoved the carriage door open and bounded down the two short stairs. Standing tall, I used our two-foot height difference to my advantage and loomed over her with a menacing glare. "If you want to keep your tongue, you will never refer to my adviser in that way ever again."

I expected the human to cower away from me, her eyes to go to the ground where they belonged, but once more she defied me. Her eyes twinkled with amusement, and her lips ticked up at the edges. "Why? Jealous?"

"Of Finch?" I scoffed and crossed my arms, jerking my head to the side. "No. Never."

She shrugged. "There's no need to be. I'm sure you have plenty of admirers." I turned my gaze back toward her as she shifted her bundle from one arm to the other. "There have to be women out there who like guys like you. Somewhere. Out there." She jerked her chin toward the town and beyond as I snarled.

Leaning down so our noses were inches from touching, I bit out, "I'll have you know that women fawn over me. They throw themselves at my feet as I walk past and beg to be in my bed."

"I'm sure they do." She nodded her head with a hint of a smile on her lips. "Where do you want me to put my stuff?"

Throwing my head back, I resisted the urge to let out a beastly roar of frustration. Instead, I pointed a finger at the box on the back of the carriage. "There."

"Thanks." She skipped passed me, not all aware of how close she was from being ripped to shreds by the monster lurking inside of me.

I watched her struggle to get her bag into the box with my arms crossed and a smirk on my lips. The box was far too high for her to reach, and she was too short to do anything but hop up and down as she tried to get the lid open.

Sighing in frustration, she glanced my way a sheepish grin on her lips. "Care to give me a hand?"

I opened my mouth to give her a resounding no when Finch appeared, looking a bit disheveled. My adviser didn't even stop beside me but hurried to the human's side and picked up her bag with a grin. "Here, allow me."

The human thanked him, her eyelashes fluttering flirtatiously.

My jaw tightened until it might break from the strain. As they chit-chatted about the journey to the palace, my anger only grew. This was not going as planned.

"The kitchen is nothing like you have back home, I assure you." Finch continued, delighted at making the human grin and giggle. "You will have so much space that you won't know what to do with yourself."

"What about the other cooks?" She chewed on her lower lip. "Will they be okay with a..." She leaned her head toward his, lowering her voice to my agitation. "... newbie invading their territory?"

For a moment, I thought she was going to say human, but that was ridiculous. We had humans working all over the palace. It wouldn't be anything new. If anything, they would be happy to have another one of their kind to work besides, but I didn't tell her that.

Finch smiled mischievously. "Oh, they might give you a hard time at first, but I'm sure that if you just feed them some of your pie, they'll be putty in your hands. His Majesty certainly seemed most taken by it."

My eyes widened and then narrowed on Finch who winked in my direction.

"Really?" The human's gaze moved over to me with a hopefulness in her eyes. "You really liked it?"

"Tell her how much you enjoyed her pie, Your Majesty." Finch smirked. He added on the title though he rarely did it out of the public eye.

My fingers itched to wrap around his neck and squeeze for putting me in such a position but then I paused. A slow wicked grin slid over my lips as I peered down at the human woman before me.

"No, I won't," I utterly coldly. "There was nothing I liked about your pie. Or your quiche." Not a flat out lie because I had loved every single bite I had taken. There was no like to it.

The human gasped in surprise as Finch frowned at me in disapproval. Tears welled in the human's eyes and I suddenly felt guilty.

"I knew it. I'm such a fuck up." She shook her head the few brown strands falling into her face.

I stared at her in horror, my eyes widening and then going from the crying human to Finch and back. This woman had faced me down without fear and now she cries? What the hell?

"Stop crying already, geez." I pulled a handkerchief from my pocket and shoved it in her direction. "It wasn't that bad."

"Really?" She took it from me and blew her nose loudly. Sniffling, she peered up at me beneath those dark lashes hopefulness in her voice. "You didn't just pick me because you just wanted to be done with it. You really like my cooking?"

I frowned at her reasoning and then shook my head. "No, I didn't pick you to be done with it though now that I think of it, I did get out of tasting all those pies." I swallowed thickly against the likelihood of what would have happened had I been subjected to that very thing. My stomach churned at the very thought.

"Oh, thank you!" the human squealed seconds before she threw herself at me, hugging my middle like her life depended on it.

My hands went up in the air not wanting to touch her or knowing what the hell was going on. I cast a helpless look to Finch who only watched with amusement.

"You have no idea how much this means to me." the human continued her voice muffled in my abdomen. "Everyone said you were a tyrant, a bully, and I'd be an idiot to want to work for the palace, but I knew it would be worth it. I just knew it."

My brows bunched together. Well, I couldn't have that.

Grabbing her by the shoulders, I pushed her into Finch's hands. "You misunderstand me. I didn't choose you because I liked your food. I choose you..." I leaned in, a cruelness curling my lips as I lowered my voice to a rumbling growl. "I choose you because I need a new toy, and you look like a challenge. One I'd love to break."

Chapter 4

Ericka

MY HEART SHUTTERED IN my chest at the king's words. It took me several seconds to recover from my shock to get more than a gasping sound out of my mouth.

"Come again?" I arched a brow. Surely, I'd heard him wrong. There was no way the king has specifically chose me just so he could mess with me. I wasn't that interesting. Ask anyone. They'd tell you, 'Ericka Burner is the most uninteresting person on the planet. Besides, the fact that she is a walking hazard waiting to happen and can't bake anything but two items to save her life.' They would say that. They actually have said that on more than one occasion. Story of my life.

However, no one would have ever thought I would garner the new fae king's attention simply by being a klutzoid. He must need his head examined.

King Balefire's lips curled further into a malicious smile, his eyes twinkling with pleasure, no doubt at my reaction. He'd been trying to rile me up for a few minutes now, but I was used to people like him. People who needed to feel better about themselves by stepping all over someone else. I grew up with a whole village of them. Nothing he could say would have made me react. Bullies lived off of the reaction of their victims and I was nobody's victim. Except I only thought I wasn't. Now, from the way he watched me like a lion who'd caught a mouse and was having way too much playing with it, I wasn't so sure.

Instead of answering my question, Balefire turned his eyes to his adviser, Finch. "It's time to go." Turning away from me, he bounded his large form up the few stairs into the carriage and dropped into his seat making the wooden structure shake.

I gaped after the fae and then shifted my eyes to Finch. "He isn't serious, is he?"

Finch seemed to fight back a grimace before nodding. "I'm afraid so. Don't take it personally..." he trailed off as I scoffed.

"How else am I supposed to take it?" I glared toward the open carriage door and into the shadows where the king hid. "He blatantly said he wanted me so he could fill his time fucking with me. It sounds a bit personal to me. Sure, I did hit him in the face with a pie, but was that really worth this?" I threw my hands up in the air and groaned long and loud. "I didn't even know it was him when I did it. Did I not lick his boots enough afterwards is that it? Is he so insecure he has to pick on a little nobody human?"

Finch's face as I rambled on and on became more worried by the second. His eyes flicked to the carriage and back to me as if he was expecting the king to come barreling out at any moment. Let him. If he thought he could break me, he had another thing coming. I was nobody's whipping boy, er, girl. I don't know how that goes. It's not like I'd heard it anywhere but from my parents.

I grew up in Elphame, or the otherworld as some still called it. Only the humans though. The fae would be offended if I ever called it such. My grandparents had made the move after the last great war. Unfortunately, that war had left the majority of the human world in ruins. The sky had been slashed red from some kind of explosion. I didn't know all the details. The humans who lived here didn't like to talk about it. They were ashamed of how their ancestors had treated our world.

Our race might very well have been extinct had the fae not opened up their arms and homes to us. Some of the humans found our subservient existence inhumane, but we were living in their world, not ours. We couldn't expect them to trust us right off the bat. Especially since we could lie, and they couldn't. It would take centuries for them to trust us enough to let us be a part of their government or have a say in anything that happened in Elphame. At least, we were able to have a say in our own lives where we lived.

For the most part, the fae left us alone. We went about our lives how we would have back in the human world. We had representatives we elected to run the towns, and we found jobs in our respective trades. Some worked in the homes of fae, like I was about to do, some preferred to only work with humans. The fae were the same way. Not all of them despised us, and many of them treated us fairly well.

Really, it could be worse.

"Are you coming or not?" Balefire's gravelly voice called from inside the carriage jerking my attention away from Finch once more. "Time is wasting away, and the way I hear it, you humans don't have much of it."

With a tight frown, I stepped toward the carriage only for Balefire to call out once more. "Not in here. In front."

My eyes darted to the front of the carriage where the driver sat and it's no handle or strap seat. Chancing a look at Finch, who gave me an apologetic smile, I walked toward the front of the carriage, my legs shaky beneath me. Finch was there at my side when I struggled to climb up to the tall seat. One hand on my elbow and a boost of strength and I was in my seat. At least, there was a cushion on it.

Giving Finch a grateful smile, I turned to the fae beside me. Four long sinewy arms held the reigns of the horses attached to the carriage. They were encased in a long silvery coat, its sleeves ending at the elbow. The head that angled in my direction had large black eyes with no iris that blinked at me with interest. The fae had little hair, and what it did have was short and pale, almost as translucent as its skin. The mouth that smiled at me was paper thin and gave me a full razor-sharp grin.

"Greetings. I'm Cailean," the fae said in a surprisingly low-pitched voice.

"I'm--"

"What's the hold up?" A banging on the roof made me jump in place, and without delay, Cailean clicked his reigns. We jolted to a start. My fingers curled around the edge of the seat, digging in until I felt the wood beneath the cushion. My jaw clenched, and I forced myself to take long deep breaths.

"Are you alright?" Cailean asked, his head turning in my direction. I didn't take my eyes off the road and watched him out of my peripherals.

"Fine." I gritted out and then gasped when we hit a bump, my nails breaking in the wood I had a death grip on.

"You don't look fine...?"

"Ericka," I bit out.

"Ericka." He nodded and then slowed the horses to a trot. Slow enough for me to relax my hands slightly, but I didn't let go of the seat. "Have you never ridden before?"

Before I could answer, Balefire growled out. "Why are we slowing?"

Angling his head, at least I assumed Cailean was a he, toward the back of the carriage, he answered, "The horses need to realign."

Accepting the answer, Balefire didn't say anything else.

I cocked a brow in question. "I thought you couldn't lie?"

"Not outright," Cailean gave me a sardonic smile, "but Fable was leaning to the right, so it wasn't quite one."

I nodded in understanding. I was warned before I left that the fae were tricky. Even if they told the truth, you never took it as the complete truth. They would trick you with every breath they took, and you would never know it.

"Thank you." I sighed and settled back into the seat. "To answer your earlier question, I don't do well on carriages or horses for that matter. Anything really that I could fall off of."

Cailean laughed, a gurgling sound. "A bumbler, eh?"

I flushed and lifted my shoulders. "All my life."

He hummed and turned his attention back to the road. The countryside around us was gorgeous. It was nothing like back in the bog. Large trees of green and crystal lined the roads. The roads themselves made of pink and purple bricks that glimmered and shined with an internal light. I would never know all the mysteries that were Elphame, not in my lifetime in any case.

However, as much beauty as there was around me, I knew there were far many more dangers, unknown and mostly unseen. There were creatures who hid in the shadows and would kill you before you even knew you'd been in danger.

My eyes slid back over to Cailean, and I chewed my lower lip. I wanted to know what he was, but you weren't supposed to ask. It was considered extremely rude, and the last thing I wanted was to offend one of my only allies.

"Kelpie."

"Huh?" I cocked my head to the side.

A small tilt of his lips drew my eyes. "You were wondering how to ask what I was without offending me. I'm a kelpie."

"How did you know that?" I gaped at him and filed away what a kelpie looked like. We didn't get many kelpies in the bog. Mostly trolls and the occasional ballybog. Most fae didn't want to be around the stench and mud that covered everyone and everything. You wouldn't catch a brownie within ten miles of Boggsville. Not on purpose.

Cailean shifted his eyes from the road to me and then back. "You aren't the first human to wonder. We kelpies don't usually stray very far from the water, but I'd always been more comfortable on land than in the ocean."

My mouth gaped and then a tiny giggle that I quickly suppressed with my hand came out. "That's unusual."

"We all have our burdens to bear." Cailean nodded and shrugged a shoulder. "Mine happens to be a kelpie mother and an elven father. He was afraid of water as well."

"How did that work out?"

A sad look crossed his face. "They live separately now, though my mother visits on occasion."

I hummed but didn't ask anything further. We came around a bend, and I sucked in a breath of awe. The palace was everything I'd heard it was and more. Tall towers of shimmering white and gold stood high above us. Windows filled with multicolored glass shone in the light and almost blinded me. A large wall surrounded the palace, the stones the color of a newborn baby in its pinkish and grey hues. It separated the palace from the road leading back into the village and the woods around us. The gate in the middle of the wall, white and gleaming, had sharp teeth which raised as the guard above saw us approaching. Clearly, they knew the king's carriage regardless of any markings on it.

The anxiety from the ride faded and was replaced by excitement and wonder. I struggled to take everything in as we moved down the streets. The stone here was the same pink and purple hue as the main road, but the buildings leading up to the main part of the palace was every color of the rainbow. Yellow cottages and green bungalows lined the streets, bunched together tightly as if to make as much room as possible for everyone.

I knew people lived in the houses surrounding the palace, but I'd never expected so many. I would think the royals wouldn't want anyone that close to them. Then again, the servants had to have somewhere to live.

"The yellow homes are those of the fae nobility." Cailean pointed out with a nod of his head. "The purple for the fae servants in the main parts of the palace. The green belongs to the fae servants who work the other parts of the palace, those that don't require interaction with the royal family."

"And the red houses?" I pointed to the section of red that stood alone from the others. "Who do they belong to?"

"The humans," Cailean answered on a gruff note. "As you can tell, the fae want to know exactly where your kind are at all times and that includes when you're sleeping."

I stared at the red houses, the color dark and deep. The color of blood. Did they really think so badly of us? And if so, why employ us at all? And finally, why the hell was I there?

Shifting uncomfortably in my seat, I forced my eyes to the front. I would worry about it later. If the king had anything to say about it, I'd be sleeping on the streets. No need to worry before I knew for sure.

Cailean lead the carriage to the side of the palace where a fae man stood with a matching silvery coat and periwinkle blue scales lining his skin. His pupils were slitted and the iris a deep yellow-purple. Those eyes glanced at me for a moment with curiosity before turning back to Cailean.

"New meat?"

With a grim expression, Cailean jerked his head towards me. "Leave her alone. I can tell the king already has his eye on this one. No need to add to her burden."

This peaked the fae's interest even more, but something in his face showed that he pitied me now more than anything. Uncomfortable under his gaze, I moved to get off the seat, but the ground was too far away from me. I ended up with my legs dangling from the side of the carriage. As I sucked in a breath to steal myself to let go, an annoyed sigh came from behind me, and large warm hands encircled my waist.

"You're going to get yourself killed before I can even have a chance to have my fun with you."

Balefire's words rumbled through me as I fell back against him.

My spine stiffened, and for a moment, I didn't breathe before scrounging up my courage and spinning on him. "Then maybe you should have thought of that before picking me. There were plenty of others who would be delighted to be the source of your amusement. I'm not one of them."

I sniffed and spun on my heel, ignoring the gaping servants surrounding the carriage as I made to grab my bag which someone had already unpacked from the back of the carriage. Picking it up, I smiled sweetly at Finch.

"Where do you want me?"

Finch, dumbfounded, shot a wary eye to Balefire and then back to me before clearing his throat. "This way. We need to get your housing set up first, then we can tour the castle."

"No."

Our heads whipped in Balefire's direction. Mine in annoyance and the rest a mixture of fear and curiosity.

Finch frowned. "What do you mean no? I suppose we could do the tour first then find housing but it's near dinner time and I would think you'd want to--"

"No, she will live here." Balefire crossed his arms over his massive chest, his eyes glittering with mischief. "In the palace. I want to have her in shouting distance."

I paled. In shouting distance? When the king had said he planned on breaking me, he hadn't been kidding. I wouldn't even get a moment of peace if I was that close to him. Finch clearly agreed with me.

"I'm not sure that is a good idea. The others..." He trailed off when he noticed we had an audience and then straightened. "We don't want to show favoritism."

A full-toothed smile filled half of Balefire's face, but none of it was kind. "Exactly." Without another word, he spun and left us the servants scattering out of his way as he passed by.

Speechless, I watched him leave, my mouth opening and closing like a kelpie out of water. Except now that I'd met an actual kelpie out of water, that figure of speech didn't really work anymore. I turned a pleading gaze to Finch.

"He's not serious, is he?" I asked. "I can't live here. In the palace. I'm human. They'll kill me." I eyed the fae servants around me. They were already filling with animosity and distrust. So much for making friends.

Sighing as he shook his head, Finch placed a hand on my shoulder and steered me toward the palace. "Unfortunately, once His Majesty has an idea in his head it's near impossible to change it. We'll just have to make the best of it. Come along."

Clutching my bag to my chest, I allowed him to lead me into the palace only briefly gaping at the interior which was even more breathtaking than the exterior. The chandelier glowed like a million starbursts and flowers decorated everything. In light of the king's personality, it was pretty funny to see such feminine decor. It certainly didn't scream Balefire.

We marched through the palace and up a wide staircase which nearly spanned the length of the entryway. The banister made up of white vines and gorgeous purple flowers brushed against my fingers as I held on trying my best not to smash any of the foliage.

I never felt more eyes on me than that moment, not even when I'd caused that fire back in Boggsville. It's not my fault that they'd let me near the bonfire during the harvest. They should know better than to trust me with rekindling the fire. I was a hazard to myself just by walking down the street. Giving me a weapon was just asking for trouble.

The eyes following me now were filled with the same mixture of emotions I'd gotten back home. Horror, disbelief, and finally anger. I forced myself to walk tall and proud, not letting their looks bother me as I was taken through the maze of hallways. They were so immense and complex that I quickly gave up trying to memorize right now. We stopped before a large door made of vines and flowers melded together to make a solid piece of wood. The door handle was clear crystal and turned with ease. Finch pushed the door open and gestured inside.

"Here you are." Finch stepped to the side and didn't enter the room with me. "Someone will be by in a bit to show you the kitchen."

"I thought you were going to give me a tour?" I stepped into the room and turned back to him, my brows furrowed. I didn't want Finch to leave just yet, to leave me alone in this strange place.

"Unfortunately, no." Finch's lips pinched into a sad smile. "Don't worry. You'll be fine."

"Promise?" Hope etched my voice. He must believe I'll be okay if he said it. He couldn't lie.

Lacing his fingers behind him, Finch inclined his head to me. "You will come to no physical harm, I promise." Then he was gone.

I twisted my eyes back to the room and scanned my new home. No physical harm, huh? There was a lot of grey area in that statement. Enough to have me building a wall back around my heart.

Let Balefire do his worst. I'd be ready.

Chapter 5

Balefire

A LONG-AGGRAVATED SIGH came pouring out of me as I tossed my pen on my desk. Dragging a hand over my face, I slumped back in my chair. I couldn't focus on any of my paperwork. There was an uprising of troll wreckage on the south border near the Summer Court. Queen Tatiana was riding my ass about getting them under control before they crossed into her fields.

It wasn't my fault the trolls were in heat. They had to do their mating dance somewhere.

I cringed and tried to shake off the thought of the large hairy creatures shaking their butts and swinging their cocks in the air like a windmill. Nobody needed to see that crap, and I'd never gotten it out of my head after the one time I'd accidentally walked into one of those mating dances.

I shuddered in revulsion and had to get that image out of my head. Right now. My eyes moved around my office, a large room with walls of books lining almost every inch of it. The only place to sit beside my desk was a tall, plush dark red chair which had been placed meticulously on a deep brown rug next to the fireplace at the exact distance to not be too cold nor too hot. It kept unwanted distractions from staying around longer than necessary.

At times like this, my mind would drift to a book to read, this time it slid over to the mirror on my desk. It wasn't a large mirror. No, it was one of those handheld ones with a long ornate handle of gold decorated in vines and flowers. It had been my mother's, and she'd given it to me when I became the king.

"So, you never forget where you came from," she'd told me with a kiss to my cheek that had made me scowl at her even though my heart had warmed inside. She never did care about who was watching. Sometimes, I wished I'd be more like her.

Picking up the mirror, I peered into the surface and wondered what my parents were up to, but it wasn't their image that poured out of the surface. It was the human, Ericka Burner.

Her shirt sleeves were folded up to the elbow, and her dark mahogany hair was once more dragged up into a messy bun on top of her head. She scrubbed rigorously at a large cast iron cauldron, so deep that half of her arm disappeared each time she reached into the cauldron.

The left side of my lip ticked up. While I might have a kingdom to run, I still had enough time to send a message to the head cook. Jasmine was a water nymph, and she had no problem with my request to give Ericka as many menial tasks as possible and to never let her near the oven or cooking areas.

I had to give the human credit. She was far more stubborn and resilient than I had thought before. It'd been four days, and still, the human had not complained once about the tasks that had been given to her. She'd been given work from washing the dishes to scrubbing the floors. Once, they even had her organizing the utensils in a precise and ridiculous pattern before 'accidentally' knocking it over, so she had to start all over again. I was sure she would have quit by now or at least run to Finch to tell. But nothing came from the girl. Not one complaint.

It was starting to irritate me. I'd have to find something even worse for her. Hard labor apparently wasn't doing it.

A snort of a laugh poured out of me. Somehow, the human caused a collision while standing in one spot. Several of the human and fae servants glared at her in annoyance as they helped each other to their feet, while Ericka gave a sheep shrug of apology.

"There you are."

Finch's voice made me jump in place, and I quickly sat the mirror face down on my desk.

Picking up my pen again, I pretended to be reading over the new policies for the troll's mating rituals.

"This is my office," I muttered. "Where else would I be?"

Finch eyed the mirror on my desk and then sniffed. "Certainly not where you're supposed to be. Did you forget what today was?"

I cocked my head to the side as I tried to bring to memory what he was talking about. "I cannot think of anything pressing at this moment."

Just then a short, pudgy fae came barreling in behind Finch. A tinkerer fae with small beady eyes and brown hair that stuck up in all directions, he pulled a pocket watch from his vest, a vest that was on the verge of popping its buttons at any moment and scowled.

"Your Majesty was supposed to meet with the Fall Court's ambassador's daughter twenty minutes ago," the tinkerer yelped.

My nose scrunched up in distaste. "Oh, that." I sighed and sat back in my chair, waving a hand. "Can't you just handle it, Randolf? Isn't that your job as the head of the council? Why do I have to be there? It's not like it's the ambassador himself."

Randolf rolled his eyes, his hands on his round hips. "You know very well that it isn't my job. And the reason she is here is to meet you. As a potential bride."

I lifted the mirror and thought of the fae in question. The surface shimmered and then a tall willowy woman with a meek expression appeared. She was pretty enough, I supposed, but just looking at her made me want to yawn. Putting the mirror back down, I shook my head.

"Tell her I'm not interested but thank you for coming."

Randolf gasped with a hand to his chest. "I will do no such thing. Lady Nico came all this way to meet you. Not me. I will not be your patsy."

"You will because I told you to." My eyes narrowed on the larger fae before me and my voice lowered to a rumble. "Or am I not king anymore?"

This time, Finch stepped in. "Bale, really. You can't stay single forever. You need an heir to make the people feel more secure in your reign. Your father married your mother as an arranged marriage, I don't see how this is any different."

I shot him a glare which caused Finch to quiet, but he didn't stiffen. He knew me too well to be afraid of my ire. I grabbed my pen and scribbled my name on the document before me. "I'm busy."

"Not too busy to spy on Ericka, though," Finch snorted.

My pen froze in mid-air for just a millisecond before I picked up the next page. "Who?"

"Yes, who?" Randolf asked, turning his curious gaze to Finch.

With a slow grin, Finch explained to the waiting fae. "Balefire hired a new human baker."

Brows furrowed, Randolf clearly didn't see the problem which was perfectly fine with me. No need to give the wretch more ammunition against me to push the marriage deal. "And we don't trust her?"

"Oh, no." Finch shook his head with a chuckle, mirth filling his eyes as he watched me. "It's nothing like that. Bale has a crush."

My pen paused again my lips pressed into a thin line. "Where would you get an idea like that?"

Finch lifted a shoulder and dropped it. "Well, why else would you pick the worst cook of them all just to pick on her?"

I opened my mouth to deny that very thing, but Finch beat me to it.

"And don't think I don't know what you're doing to that poor girl. You should see how worn out she is by the time she gets back to her room, a room that you insisted be near yours. Or have you not even noticed her nearness?"

I had in fact. While I didn't meet her in the hallway, that would be ludicrous, I watched her walk back to her room and collapse on her bed every night. She rarely wasted time to bathe before falling asleep. I assumed she bathed at some point during the night. She was fresh faced and ready to start the day by the time I woke up.

However, Finch's chastisement made guilt eat at my stomach. Perhaps I had been too hard on her.

Lifting a calculating gaze to Finch, I shoved my chair back and stood. "Very well. Randolf." The tinkerer stiffened to attention. "Tell Lady Nico that I am unable to meet her at this time, but I would be delighted if she would join me for dinner."

"Yes, Your Majesty!" Pleasure surged over his face and Randolf nodded his head eagerly. "Right away." Randolf hurried away, but Finch stayed standing where he was, suspicion lining his face.

"What?" I barked as I grabbed a pen to scribble a note to the head cook. I would have guests tonight, and there had to be an adequate banquet prepared. I couldn't present myself like some kind of savage.

"And what of Ericka?"

"What of her?" I bristled, not wanting him to see past my hard exterior. He simply stared at me until I grumbled. "Fine. I'll let up on her. In fact," a slow smile crawled up my face, "I have just the job for her."

"Oh, no." Finch took a step closer to my desk. "I know that look. That isn't a 'I'm going to give the girl a break' look. That's an 'I have something even worse up my sleeve' look."

I forced myself not to smile. The fae knew me too well. Instead, I gaped at him in mock horror.

"I would do no such thing," I scoffed. "Besides, you said no more hard labor. I hardly think joining my guests and me for dinner is hard work."

Finch's eyes narrowed as he watched my face. His lips pinched into a displeasing frown, but I ignored him as I made for the door. Before I stepped out, Finch asked, "What's your endgame?"

I stiffened and twisted back around. "What do you mean?"

"I mean, what's the point of all of this?" Finch urged me to answer him with a pleading gesture. "You are hardly the type to take on unneeded distractions. And don't try to tell me you're bored or are teaching her a lesson, because I know that's a load of shite."

My brows shoved together as I puckered my mouth to one side. "I don't know what you are talking about. She disrespected me in front of the villagers. Of course, this is to teach her a lesson. What else could it be?"

"I'm not sure, but it's not like you." Finch stroked his jaw in thought. "I was only kidding about the crush, but the way you are acting is starting to make me wonder. Do you care for Ericka?"

I gaped at him for real this time. "Me? Care for a human woman? That's laughable. No, inconceivable. I have killed people for less."

"No, you haven't." Finch snorted. "You forget, you tell me everything. You haven't killed anyone that didn't deserve it, and this hardly counts." He placed his hands on his hips and tapped a foot. "And what's this nonsense with Lady Nico? You shouldn't give the sweet girl hope for the sake of torturing Ericka. Her father will not be as understanding."

"Pfft." I waved him off and turned back to the door. "I can handle Marcus. You just worry about getting Ericka the right clothes for the job. I have a reputation to uphold after all."

I held a hand to my chest and lifted my chin before marching out of the room. The sight of Finch's incredulous face made me laugh all the way to my bedroom.

Chapter 6

Ericka

I GROANED AS I finished up the last dish in the sink and surveyed my body. My hands hurt. My back. My neck. Oh gods, everything ached. Even my toes. How in the world was that possible?

They told me back home that working at the palace would be vastly different from working in Boggsville but this? This was beyond anything I could have imagined.

I knew from the beginning that living in the palace would make the other servants wary of me. It was clearly favoritism in the worst way possible. Nobody greeted me on my first day. Nobody even introduced themselves to me. The only person who talked to me was the head cook, Jasmine, a water nymph with a voluptuous figure and pouty lips. She wasn't exactly mean to me, but she was short, stern. Never gave me room to argue or ask questions, simply pushed me toward a task and then criticized every moment of it.

"How can you possibly be trusted to make the king's pies if you can't even wash a dish correctly?" she pointed out this morning when I came down to the kitchen. I'd already cleaned the floors and aligned all the utensils just so only to have them ruined in the next five minutes. That one was hard to swallow, but I did so without complaint.

I couldn't help but wonder if everyone in the kitchen had the same tasks thrust upon them when they first arrived, or if this trial was caused by the king's favoritism? It certainly couldn't be anything I'd done. I'd only just arrived, and I'd done nothing but offer kindness to those around me.

"Burner!" Jasmine called out, jerking me out of my thoughts.

I slowly turned, holding back a wince as the ache in my bones. "Yes, ma'am?"

"You're done for the day." Her dark blue hair fell into her pale face as she gestured a hand in my direction.

I frowned at her. "But it's only two. We still have dinner to--"

"Are you questioning me?" The nymph cut me off with a glare, her hands on her apron covered hips. "Are you head cook?"

"No, ma'am," I quickly jumped in, holding my hands up.

"I don't know how they did things back in Boggsville," she spat the word as if it tasted rotten in her mouth before grabbing me by the elbow and pulling me toward the door, "but here, you do as you're told and be happy for a place to lay your head."

My eyes shifted around me as I let her pull me through the kitchen. All the other servants, a mixture of fae and humans, watched with curious expressions. Some seem to pity me, but others seemed to revel in the way Jasmine was treating me. Like she was putting me in my place.

I tried not to let myself believe that was the case. I was sure she was just doing her job, so I pushed down my hurt and allowed her to push me out of the kitchen. Jasmine nudged me and jerked her head towards the stairs.

"Go to your room and don't come back here until tomorrow morning."

With that, she spun on her heel and went back to prepping for dinner.

My brows drew together as I rubbed my arm where her nails had bit into it and chewed on my lower lip. I didn't want to disobey, but I couldn't help but wonder if I'd done something wrong. Did I wash the dishes incorrectly? Or maybe it was a puddle of water several of the others had slipped in earlier that I hadn't noticed I was making?

I cast another worried and regretful look toward the kitchen before moving toward the stairs. I'd barely gotten two steps when the whispering started. I usually ignored the talking behind my back. Servants were notorious gossips, so I was used to it by now, but something they said made my hand pause on the banister.

"That poor girl," a voice I recognized to belong to a human woman named, Becca, tisked. "I'm all for making sure no one gets a big head, but this is just so wrong."

"Shush," another voice said. It belonged to a brownie named Tryst who had been the one to bump into my painstakingly organized utensils. "The king has made his orders clear. Who are we to question him?"

My mouth fell open in surprise. Seriously? It was Balefire's fault I was getting treated like crap?

"But why? Why this girl? She's human for one and for another she seems like she'd be really nice," Becca argued, her voice going high with distress. "I don't want to lose a chance at a friendship because the king has a bug up his ass."

"You hold your tongue," Jasmine snapped, and a gasp of pain from Becca made me wince. I felt her pain. Jasmine's nails were no joke. "You do not speak of the king in such a manner. In fact, you shouldn't speak of him at all unless you'd like to be fed to his pet dragon, Shirazan."

The whole kitchen went silent at that threat, and I hurried up the stairs. I'd heard rumors of the dragon. A large fae creature with wings that were the length of ten men and scales so hard that they could scratch a diamond. Shirazan was said to breathe fire, and the king was known to send her to eat anyone who defied him. I wasn't sure how valid those rumors were because I had yet to hear of anyone who had actually seen or been eaten by her. So, until I actually heard something legit, I wasn't too worried about it.

Besides, if the king was behind my hard days, then he was living up to his promise of torturing me to put me in my place. I highly doubted he would feed me to a dragon any time soon, and I would make sure that it wouldn't come to that.

Stomping up the stairs, my jaw tensed as I thought of how I could get the kitchen staff off my back and get back at the king. At least the servants seemed to be on my side. Well, those who weren't terrified of the king in any case. I surely could win them over somehow. I might be a klutz, but more people liked me than not back home, and I would like to think it was for my winning personality and not just my decadent pies. The gods knew it wasn't for any of my other cooking.

I snort laughed to myself as I walked down the hallway toward my room. I tried to think of today as a blessing in disguise. I could take a long bath, something I hadn't had time to do since I'd arrived. I could find the library, renowned for its vast collection, and then take an early dinner before going to bed.

Happy for my plan, a skip appeared in my steps. I hummed a little tune and skipped the rest of the way. At least, until I was brought up short by the figure waiting by my bedroom door.

Finch.

His dark hair curled around his shoulders, and his eyes were focused on the ground in front of him. That combined with the way his arms were crossed over his chest made him seem displeased with something. Frustrated.

"Lord Finch?" I slowly started for my room once more and stopped before him. "What are you doing here?" but then quickly added, "Not that you can't be here. I mean, this is more your home than mine. I supposed it would only make sense that you would be here."

Thankfully, Finch saved me from myself by placing a hand on my shoulder. Then he led me to my room and opened the door for me.

"Please, don't worry yourself, Ericka. You aren't in trouble. I promise." He offered me a broad smile that was just this side of too big. He was hiding something, but I couldn't put my finger on it.

When we stepped into my room, my suspicions grew. Inside stood a slim fae woman with a measuring tape in one hand and a pair of scissors in the other. She had one other set of arms beneath the first set, and her golden eyes were locked onto my form, measuring me with her eyes.

Finch ushered me over to the woman. "This is Odette. She will be fitting you for your new uniform."

"Uniform?" I frowned and looked down at the grayish blue skirt I wore with a long-sleeved white shirt. There wasn't a dress code for the kitchen, but this was what I'd worn back home for work, so I figured it would be okay. Apparently, I was mistaken.

Guessing my confusion, Finch chuckled. "What you are wearing is fine usually, but the king has some special guests tonight and would like you to help serve dinner."

At the mention of the king, my teeth ground together. "And he wants me to look the part, does he?"

Taken aback by my biting tone, Finch's eyes widened before he recovered himself, frowning slightly. "Yes, in a manner of speaking. We made sure your daily work was covered so this won't put you behind or anything."

"Oh, how nice of him." My voice oozed sarcasm as I turned from Finch to Odette. She stood with her back straight and her face even straighter. If she had any thoughts about my words or the way that Finch blanched, she didn't show it. Woman had a killer poker face.

"Yes, well." Finch cleared his throat and then adjusted the tie of his suit. Turning to Odette, he inclined his head. "This is Ericka. His Majesty would like her outfitted for tonight's dinner. Please make sure she is properly prepared."

Nodding to Finch, Odette gave a half courtesy before turning those golden eyes back onto me. Without warning, she was on me. Lifting an arm, wrapping the tape around my middle, and generally poking and prodding me. I gasped and glowered at her with she cupped my breasts through my shirt to get the size of them.

"Well, I will be heading back." Finch shifted uncomfortably in place as he coughed into his hand. "Dinner is at seven. You will need to report to the dining room about six. If you have any questions, Luke will help you."

Before I could ask him, who was Luke and where could I find him, Finch hurried out of the room. If I didn't know any better, I'd say he was embarrassed by the way Odette manhandled me, or it could just be the guilt radiating off him. Finch hadn't been lying per say. He believed everything he was telling me, but that wasn't much. To keep from lying was probably why he was keeping his mouth shut and making me wait to ask Luke. I glanced over my shoulder at Odette who was checking my hem line.

"You don't happen to know what's going on, do you?" I asked.

Odette kept her gaze on my body and for a moment, I thought she wasn't going to answer me. Then a small voice, barely above a whisper, came from her lips.

"Keep him entertained."

"Huh?" I arched to hear her better and got smacked on the leg for my effort. Wincing, I straightened back up. "You mean the king?"

"You have his interest, good," Odette continued. "Keep it that way. If you value your life."

Her ominous words only made me frown harder. "I don't want his interest. I certainly don't plan on keeping him entertained. I'm a person, not a thing for his amusement."

"Oh, dear human." She sniffed a laugh. "You are most amusing. Just keep doing what you're doing, and you will be fine."

I huffed, crossed my arms over my chest, and then got pinched for it in the process. Muttering under my breath of all the ways I would show the king how I amusing I was, I let Odette do her job without further movement.

It was just ridiculous. Didn't the king have anything better to do? Weren't there women for him to woo or courts to wage war with? Who had time to mess with a lowly human? I certainly never had that much time on my hands. I spent most of my days working in my parents' shop and then we had to prep the dough for the next day's bread. Any spare time I had went into reading or taking a bath. I certainly didn't have much time for dating. Not that anyone had caught my eye.

There was one human boy once when I was sixteen who had been interested in me. Well, I'd been interested in him as well, but more in a curious way. He liked to watch me bake and smelled like dandelions and sweet grass. I think he worked in the fields. He came around for a while never asking me out or even talking to me more than just to say hello. Then, one day, when I had the courage to talk to him myself, I had one of my accidents. Safe to say that after catching his shirt on fire, he didn't come around anymore.

"Done." Odette stepped away from me, holding a knee length dress of crimson in her hands. It had long sleeves and a scoop neck. The material was smooth and shimmery beneath my fingers. A ribbon in a slightly lighter shade of red wrapped around the middle of it, no doubt to tie in the back when worn.

"Oh, Odette. It's lovely." My mouth formed an o as I praised it. "How did you make it so fast?"

"It's what I do." Odette shrugged. "I can create any kind of clothing in a matter of moments. I just need the right measurements. You're easy. Now, dressing the king's head of council..." She covered her mouth as she let out a little giggle. "That's another story."

I smiled back at her before taking the dress over to the bed. "Thank you so much. I love it. I just wish it wasn't to serve him." I made a face that caused Odette to laugh softly.

"Things aren't always the way we want them to be," she told me mysteriously as she walked toward the bedroom door. She paused and looked back at me. "That goes the same for people, but sometimes they're exactly what we need."

Curious at her words but unable to ask her what she meant before she left, I glanced up at the clock. I still had a few hours before I had to be down in the dining room, just enough time to take a long and relaxing bath. I was going to need it for the night ahead. I just knew it.

Chapter 7

Ericka

I TUGGED AT THE sleeves of my dress, fidgeting in place. How did I get stuck with a job like this? I was a baker not a server. I'd never served anyone in my life, let alone a bunch of royals.

Sighing dejectedly, I pulled at the sleeves once more.

"Are you alright?" Luke asked, his face the image of concern.

My eyes moved from the dining table currently being set for six and slid over to the faun. He had curly brown hair with two small horns on either side of his head. Pointed ears peaked out from the curls and a pert nose poked out right in the middle of his face. He was cute for a faun. Luke sure filled out the button-down shirt and vest that matched my crimson dress, though I wasn't sure if I'd ever be able to get passed the hooved feet and furry legs. I liked hair but that much just teased the line of bestiality for me. Still, there were women who loved it. Faun were big womanizers. It was their chocolatey voice and music I was sure.

"Oh, don't worry about me." I waved him off with a sheepish smile. "I'm fine."

He gave me a mischievous wink and leaned next to me where we stood against the dining room wall. "Not your usual scene huh?"

"Is it that obvious?" Laughing nervously, I scratched the side of my face.

"I bet you are wondering the same as everyone else." He shrugged.

"And what's that?"

"Why the king requested your presence, of course." He glanced back to the table being set up, his arms crossed over his chest. Luke was in charge of making sure everything was perfect for His Majesty. Apparently, the bastard king was as much of a pain about a fork placement as he was about everything else. Normally, I'd misalign everything just to piss him off, but I didn't want to get anyone else in trouble. I was having enough problems making friends as it was. Letting out a long drawn out breath of air, I shook my head and closed my eyes.

"I don't know why he's doing this to me," I complained. "I can hardly say I deserve it. I'm a baker for crying out loud and not even that good of one."

Luke hummed a long minute and then snapped his fingers turning to me. "Maybe he has a crush."

"What?" I screeched, a sound that caused the other workers to stop what they were doing and stare over at us. Offering an apologetic smile to the others, I then lowered my voice and turned to Luke. "Why would you think that? I threw a pie in his face. If anything, he wants to kill me. Slowly. With a butter knife."

"Well, I can't blame him." Luke chuckled in an adorable way that made the women workers all swoon as he dragged a hand through his already unruly hair. "Though it would depend on the kind of pie."

"It was blueberry," I interjected like it mattered.

"Well, in that case..." Luke grew serious, crossing his arms once more as he closed his eyes and nodded. "I would have fed you to the dragon already."

"No, you wouldn't." I giggled and nudged him on the shoulder playfully. "You love me too much."

"You think very highly of yourself, if you think I love you already."

I grinned broadly at him and arched a brow. "Don't you?"

Luke played as if he was thinking about it, shrugging one shoulder and then the other. I giggled and nudged him with my elbow again.

"Okay," he admitted. "I guess I tolerate you."

"I can't go on," I gasped and clutched my chest with both hands as if I'd been struck by an arrow. I wobbled in place, grabbing a hold of Luke's arm. " Tell the king, I--"

"Tell the King what?"

The low rumbling voice of Balefire caused the occupants of the room to freeze. Not a sound could be heard. I wasn't even sure anyone was breathing. I straightened slowly, removing my hand from Luke's arm and clearing my throat as my eyes found the bright blue eyes of the king.

Those gorgeous orbs, totally wasted on the fae man before me, held both annoyance and curiosity. Standing high above everyone else in the room, he wore a pale blue button-down shirt lined with golden brocade. The shirt fit his broad shoulders and revealed the tight muscles beneath the fabric. His tattoos peeked out beneath the collar and at his wrist. Normally, those tattoos caused those who knew what they meant to go on the defensive, but to me, they triggered a strange tingling in the pit of my stomach. I resolved to define it as resentment. Surely not interest. Not in him. He's pretty for a fae, sure, but he was also an asshole.

To Balefire's left stood Finch, his lips pressed into a severe line even as his eyes shone brightly with amusement. He was clearly trying to hold back his laughter. Finch dressed for one of his station, a shirt similar to the king's except in a deep brown, but while the king didn't wear a jacket, Finch did. It fit his form perfectly, accenting every inch of him. I could see a few of the female servants flutter their lashes in his direction once they got over the initial shock of the king's words.

Unfortunately, it seemed that everyone was waiting for my response, the king especially. So, I cleared my throat and laced my fingers in front of me as I put on my best demur smile.

"My apologies, Your Majesty. We were simply discussing how odd it is for a baker such as myself to be acting as your server. I'm not exactly qualified for the job." My words seemed to smooth out some of the feathers I'd ruffled by being here, but the king didn't find my words so appeasing.

As he stalked into the room, his lips ticked up into a smirk. Balefire stopped before his place at the table. A servant quickly rushed to his side and pulled it out for him. He ignored her, a sprite, named Lily, I think, and locked eyes on me.

"Are you questioning my decision, Miss Burner?" the king asked curtly. "Should I have allowed you to make the meal for our esteemed guests? A no-name baker with a name like Burner could hardly be trusted to not poison my guests, don't you think?"

I lifted my shoulder in a noncommittal sort of way. "I don't pretend to know what goes on in your mind, your majesty. It's obviously far above my pay grade. As for my baking skills, you yourself chose me for this position. Are you saying you don't trust your own judgement?"

I was playing with fire. I knew I was. Still, I couldn't help the condescension that poured out of my mouth. I was tired of being played a fool. He wanted to mess with me? Fine. But he better be able to take it if he's going to dish it out, and this human liked to serve hers steeping hot.

My question astounded those around me, and even Luke sucked in a surprised breath. The way they tensed and paused in their movements told me that they expected Balefire to strike me down right there. I half-hoped that he would so we could stop this game of ogre and gnome. No one liked to be the butt of a joke, least of all me.

Balefire's jaw ticked as he slowly sat in his chair and placed one hand on the table. His long index finger tapped in slow succession as he surveyed me. Finch strolled into the room further, waving the servant off who tried to pull his chair out for him to the left of Balefire. His emerald green eyes shifted back and forth between us as if trying to figure out if he should intervene. After what seemed like an eternity, the king's finger stopped tapping on the table.

"Out," he suddenly commanded in a loud, booming voice.

Instantly, the room came back to life in a frenzy. Servants bumped into each other. Plates fell to the ground as they all rushed to leave the dining room, and I moved to follow Luke out.

"Not you, Miss Burner," the king demanded.

Luke hesitated and tossed a sympathetic look over his shoulder before hurrying out of the room as well. I guess he didn't like me that much yet.

Holding back an irritated sigh, I waited for Balefire to get to the point so I could get back to work. I didn't want to listen to whatever downgrading venom was about to spill out of those gorgeous lips.

As he crossed one leg over the other, Balefire lifted a hand and gestured for me to come forward. When I hesitated, he arched a brow. I ground my teeth and curled my fingers into fists as I moved one short step at a time to the table and stopped several feet away.

"Come now, I won't bite." Balefire gave me a wolfish grin, making me think he meant the exact opposite.

With a defiant glare, I took one more step toward him and stopped again. To my satisfaction, Balefire's smile dipped slightly, and brows furrowed, he looked me over studiously.

"Why do you fight me so? Things could be so much easier for you if you simply abide by my wishes."

I snorted before I could stop myself.

"See? That right there is what I am talking about." He pointed at my face with an astonished frown. "Why is it that every other servant I've ever had has known to keep their mouths shut and their reactions to themselves? But you can't seem to keep what you're thinking off your face or your lips." His gaze dipped down to the lips in question.

The look made me squirm, but I forced myself to meet his gaze.

"Maybe because they fear you and I don't." I spoke loud and clear so that he couldn't pretend that he didn't understand me.

Finch groaned and lowered his face to his hand as he shook his head from side to side. He certainly didn't agree with my actions, but he also wasn't going to call me out on it. Balefire's reaction was the only one that mattered in any case.

I expected him to lash out, tell me that I was going to the dungeon or wherever else the fae royals sent their unwanted servants. At the least, I expected him to get angry, but when he started to laugh, I flinched back. This wasn't a little chortle, but a full-on head-back, throat-barred belly laugh. If I wasn't so shocked, I'd have found him largely attractive. That lovely blonde hair that cascaded over his shoulders. That voice that I'd only heard speak out of spite and anger came out low and rumbling, making strange things stir in my nether regions. I finally understood why some of the women might fear him, but they also wanted him... desperately.

Gulping, I took a step back as he continued to laugh for an uncomfortably long time. A sideways look at Finch told me that this was unusual for him too. The slack jawed expression and round eyes told me as much. I took several more steps back just for good measure.

As quickly as the laughing started, it stopped the second I took my last step.

"Stop." I froze at the seriousness in Balefire's voice, all the laughter now gone from it. "I do not know if you are brave or just stupid, Miss Burner, but I suppose things would get boring quickly if you were that easily broken." He flashed me a wicked grin, and my pulse jumped. I didn't know if it was from fear or... something else, but at that moment, I didn't have the time to figure it out.

Quick as lightning, Balefire's hand shot out and grabbed me by the arm. He jerked me forward until we were inches apart, then he took my chin in his hands and lifted my face up to meet his gaze. His voice lowered as if he were talking to a lover, but the words that poured from his mouth was nothing short of venomous.

"Believe me when I say this: You think you don't fear me, but I will do my best to prove you wrong." He leaned in so that his lips brushed my ear, and my heart pounded in my veins so loudly that I barely heard him as he whispered, "And I will revel in every sweet torturous moment of it."

Then he shoved me away so fast that I almost lost my footing and fell. Wouldn't that have been embarrassing? Worst yet, he turned his back on me and returned to his chair without a backward look.

"So, where are our esteemed guests?" the king asked Finch.

Finch stared at me for a long moment before clearing his throat and answering, "You told them seven. It is barely after five o'clock."

Balefire glanced over at the clock on the mantel and let out a long, drawn-out groan. "So, it is. Why are we doing this again?'

He was acting as if I weren't even in the room at all. Was this the way he treated all the other servants? As if they were invisible, and all of his food just magically appeared before him? It twisted my stomach in knots and made me want to smack him over the head at the same time. Fucking fae royalty and their lack of appreciation for those who worked for them.

"You're still here?" Balefire's eyes snapped to me. That's when I realized I was growling. I abruptly stopped, but his next words made me want to start again. "Don't you have some dishes to clean or something?"

Narrowing my eyes on him, I gave a curtsy that showed nothing but my contempt for him before storming out of the room. The soft sounds of his and Finch's conversation followed after me. When I stepped into the serving room, one room closer to the kitchen, I jolted to a stop. All eyes were on me.

I gave a weak smile and waved. "Hey."

"You're alive," Luke gasped, grabbing my hands in his and then pulling me into a hard hug. "We thought you were done for."

I struggled against his embrace and squeaked out, "Can't breathe," before he let me go.

"Oops, sorry." Luke grinned sheepishly as he released me, but he kept his hands on my shoulders. "So, what happened? How are you not dragon food right now?"

Several other servants who had pretty much ignored me before stepped closer as if they too wanted to know how I survived my encounter with the beast. Scratching the back of my head, I laughed nervously.

"It was fine. No big deal." I shrugged a shoulder. When they only watched me and waited for more, I sighed and shook my head. "I don't know. He has some weird infatuation with making my life miserable. It's like, the more I defy him, the more he wants to screw with me. I think it's all a game to him." I shrugged again. "The gods must be bored or something."

There was a collective gasp before everyone was talking at once, coming in at me from all sides.

"What's he like up close?"

"Are his eyes as sparkly as they seem?"

"Did he hit you?"

"Are you sleeping with him?"

"Uh... kind of a jerk. I guess. Not really. Hell no!" On and on they went. So many questions that they all blurred together, and I had to force myself out of the horde before I got trampled. "Look, I don't want to cause any more trouble than I already have." I moved to a serving dish and started to fill it with plates. "Why don't we get ready before His Majesty," I rolled my eyes, sticking my tongue through my teeth, which caused the group to giggle and laugh, "finds something else to complain about?"

At my insistence, everyone went back to their tasks. Some went in and out of the serving room door and back into the dining room, but I didn't dare go back in there. Not now. Luke came up to my side to help me ladle soup into bowls.

"You're playing a dangerous game, Ericka. I'd be careful if I was you."

"Believe me." I glanced up from what I was doing and gave him an incredulous smile. "It's not a game I want to be playing. He picked me for some gods forsaken reason, and I'm just trying to survive." I filled another bowl full of the simmering pumpkin soup that smelled to die for before adding a basil leaf for garnish to the center. "Maybe he'll get bored soon and find someone else to pick on."

"I doubt it." Luke snorted. "If the king is anything, it's persistent and stubborn. He won't stop until he gets what he wants." He grabbed my arm to stop me from my task, his eyes serious as they bore into mine. "If I were you, I'd just give it to him. You'll be happier for it. And safer."

A weak smile slid over my face as I placed my hand on top of his. "I wish I could, but where he is stubborn, I'm worse. I don't abide by bullies, and if the king is anything, he's the biggest bully of them all."

"He's not that bad." Rolling his eyes, Luke lifted his shoulders in a noncommittal way. "I mean, once you know to stay out of his way. Life here can be quite pleasant, if not fun."

I narrowed my eyes on him and placed a hand on my hip. "He made a laundry girl cry because she didn't iron his shirt clockwise instead of counterclockwise."

Luke winced. "Well, everyone has their quirks. Can you blame him?"

"Yes." I went back to ladling, being even more forceful than before. "Yes, I can."

"Uh... Ericka?" The sprite from earlier stuttered her long green lashes fluttering. She fiddled with her hands and ran a hand through her grass green hair. "His Majesty is asking for you."

I frowned at her and then nodded. After wiping my hands on a nearby towel, I moved toward the door.

The sprite stopped me. "And his soup."

I stopped in my tracks before turning back to the table. Picking up one of the bowls, I would be lying if I didn't say that I was more than tempted to spit in it, but I held back. With a forced smile, I turned on my heel and walked through the dining room door.

Unlike before, the table was full of guests and the room full of their chatter. There were talking about something frivolous like getting silks from the Autumn Court. I held back the urge to roll my eyes and walked slowly to the head of the table where King Balefire sat.

He didn't look my way as I stood next to him, and I waited for him to move so I could sit his bowl down. Balefire laughed at something a pretty woman to his right said before replying.

"The thing with humans is that you have you train them right or they will run all over your kingdom." His eyes flickered up to mine with a hint of a smile. "Like gnats."

Anger spiked in me, and I want to say that my hand slipped or that the bowl got too hot. But really, I wanted to do it.

I let the bowl slip from my hands and into Balefire's lap. His roar of pain and the cries from the other table occupants made my hackles go up, and before I could stop myself, I was rushing out of the door.

I was starting to think I really did have a death wish.

Chapter 8

Balefire

RAGE. UNADULTERATED RAGE POURED through my being. I stood there in the dining room before my guests and friends, shaking with that primal fury. The hot soup did not even register to my mind anymore, my anger totally overwhelming any feelings of pain.

That human. That ungrateful, petulant human woman.

How dare she? Who did she think she was? She thought she could just disrespect me in such a way and run for it?

What she did could be constituted as treason for attempting harm on me. Not that she had probably thought through it that much. I knew my comments were getting to her, and I'd said them for her benefit.

However, I hadn't expected her to step so far out of line as to dump soup on me, though I doubted the rest of the room saw it that way.

They probably thought it had been an accident, but I'd seen it. I'd seen the anger in her eyes the second before the soup slipped out of her hands. This was no accident. I wanted to throw my head back and laugh in my fury, but I couldn't, not now. Not in front of our guests.

"Are you alright, Your Majesty?" Lady Nico of the Summer Court timidly offered me a napkin as if that would help clean the hot liquid soaking into my pants at that moment.

I resisted the urge to snarl at her. Instead, I took in a long breath before turning a grateful smile her way. "Yes, thank you, Lady Nico. I apologize for the interruption to your dinner. Some servants are harder than others to train." As I spoke, Finch jumped in from my left and rushed to my side.

"Yes, it takes weeks to get a servant up to par with our standard of service. It was our mistake for putting a novice in charge of serving this evening." He shot a disapproving look in my direction which I ignored. "Please excuse us while His Majesty gets cleaned up." He pulled my chair back, but I waved him off with a barely suppressed growl.

"Oh, please don't worry on our account," Lady Nico assured us with a hand to her chest and a flutter of her lashes. "Perhaps I could help you clean up? It's the least I could do for having received us, Your Majesty."

Huh. Lady Nico had been nothing but timid and quiet the whole meal. Demure would be what I'd have described her the most. Most boring. I needed more spark to my women, not someone who would scrape and bow for my affections. Now, I saw that meekness was all a ploy. To so blatantly offer herself to my service for such an intimate task showed she had more backbone than I thought.

Unfortunately, I had other ideas.

"No, thank you, Lady Nico. I have some urgent work to attend to." I offered her a charming smile. "A leader's work is never done. Please, enjoy your meal without any further disruption." I glanced over at Luke as I spoke, which made the faun flinch.

Finch placed his hand on my back as if to guide me out of the room, but in all actuality, it was a way to remind me that I was still in public and could not lash out just yet. We walked at a fast pace out of the dining room and into the hallway. The further away from the dining room we got, the more my anger flared back to life. Servants and nobles who loitered in the hallways took one look at my face and fled. I could imagine the sight of me, but I didn't care. I only had one person on my mind right now.

The human.

I tried to change my course toward where I knew Finch had placed her, only a few rooms away from mine. A room far to lavish for a servant. I'd hoped the other servants would have tortured her more for me because of that very reason, but it seemed as if I had miscalculated my own staff's viciousness. If the human had enough spirit to dump soup on me in the middle of a public dinner, then I'd done a poor job at killing that part of her, something I would correct right now.

Some jobs you simply had to do personally.

"Hold on now," Finch stepped in front of me his hands up in between us. "You can't just go in there. Not like this. You'll kill her."

"No, I won't." I snarled and shoved him to the side, but the little pest wouldn't leave me alone.

"Yes, you will," Finch pointed out with a no-nonsense glower. He placed himself between me and the human's door, his arms crossed over his chest as if that would be enough to stop me. "Think about this for a moment. As far as anyone else is concerned, it was an accident. If word gets out that you're killing servants for the slightest offense, we'll be making our own breakfast come morning."

I paused. He had a point. I'd done well to keep my rage under control and only showing the beast inside when the need arose. Killing a human servant, though, wouldn't look good for me at all, especially for those not completely clued into what actually happened.

Grinding my teeth, I glared at the door once more and then back to Finch. "Fine. The human lives... but she must be punished."

Finch sighed in what could be called relief. He lifted his shoulders and shook his head.

"I don't know why you continue to torture the girl," he murmured. "If I'd been in her place, I'd have dumped soup on you too, but I'd have aimed for your head."

I rolled my eyes and turned on my heels to head back toward my bedroom door. I smelled of pumpkin. I hated pumpkin. Why did the cook even make this? Making a note to myself to speak with the head cook tomorrow about the menus, I pushed my bedroom door open.

Finch followed in after me, rambling something about not being so hard on the human. Pfft. Like that would happen. I would break her. It was only a matter of time.

"If you wish to punish her, make it a private punishment," Finch continued, moving over to my desk and lifting up a piece of paper to skim over. "One that doesn't involve public eyes to witness."

I wasn't worried about Finch going through my things. We had no secrets. He knew me inside and out. The good and the... ugly. Plus, I trusted him with my life. I wouldn't have made it through puberty had it not been for him. I needed him on my side, but for some reason, the human has caused this rift between us. With me on one side and Finch and her on the other. I didn't like it. Not at all.

"What do you suggest I do?" I growled, pulling my shirt over my head and tossing it toward the hamper. I missed. I worked on my boots and pants next while Finch moved across the room and picked up my discarded shirt to put it where it belonged.

"Perhaps a tedious punishment," Finch suggested. "Have her clean the gutters or run errands for the palace. Gods know that the servants hate those the most." His eyes twinkled as he thought about it, but none of those were punishments fitting for the humiliation I'd endured. I tossed my ruined pants toward the basket as well, and an idea hit me.

"No," I rumbled which caused Finch to pause and frown. "Bring her to me." A slow, malicious grin slid up my face. "She made this mess. She can clean it."

Finch gaped at me in astonishment for a moment or two before he finally said something. "You can't be serious."

"Oh, I am." I grinned even wider. Standing there nude with my hands on my hips, I stared him down. "She humiliated me. Now, it's her turn. Tit for tat."

"But, but," Finch sputtered trying to come up with some kind of response. "You have legions of women who would love to help you bathe. Willing women. In fact, Lady Nico offered that very thing.

Why do you not request her presence, instead?" My adviser tried to sway me from my decision, but I wouldn't be moved.

"Precisely," I retorted as I crossed my arms and leaned against the banister of my bed. "That human woman despises me. She wouldn't want to come within five feet of my bathing chamber. It will be the perfect form of punishment for her. She'll be humiliated and hopefully humbled into being the respectful human servant as she should be for the sake of never having to do it again."

I chuckled to myself. It really was the best punishment I could have come up with. If manual labor didn't do it, then putting her in this position would definitely do it. Perhaps I'll even suggest she bathe me regularly. My grin only grew on my face.

Finch made a disbelieving sound and my head jerked up to meet his gaze.

"You are walking a fine line here, Balefire." He shook his head with a sigh.

"Why do you say that?"

Moving toward the door, Finch glanced back at me. "So far, she has reacted in a completely surprising manner to everything you've thrown at her. I do not think she will sway from her path as easily as you do."

"You don't know women the way I do," I scoffed.

This time, it was Finch's turn to laugh. "No, Your Majesty. You don't know women the way I do."

"You're a womanizer. I would hardly call you an expert on women. Perhaps on fucking them but not on their minds or feelings." I waved him off and headed for the bathing chamber. "Leave that to me."

I could feel Finch smiling at my back, but I ignored him. Turning the knobs on the bathtub, I watched as the water poured out of the faucets. Indoor plumbing was a miraculous thing indeed. Far better than boiling water or using magic to warm my bath. I waited until the tub was halfway full then stepped into the steaming hot water.

Leaning my head back on the edge of the metal tub, I sighed. This was the life. Give me a quiet bath and I could die in bliss. I let my eyes droop down as I sunk further into the bath.

A bump on the side of the tub me jarred into a sitting position. I glared up to see Finch's smirking face, and I wiped a hand over my face to dry it.

"You're still here? I thought I sent you to get the human."

"I will." Finch beamed down at me, his hands on the edge of the tub. "I just had one question for you."

"Get on with it," I groaned in annoyance and tossed my hand in his direction. "I know you will anyway."

Finch wasn't at all hurt by my words. In fact, they only amused him more.

"I wonder, what will you do if Ericka doesn't run screaming into the night? What will you do... if she likes it?"

His words and laughter stayed with me as he walked out of the room. What if? No. She couldn't. Wouldn't. Would she?

Chapter 9

Ericka

I WAS DEAD. I was so dead. I was so completely dead that they were probably planning my funeral back home. No, they wouldn't even do that. I had shamed my family with my stupidity, so they wouldn't even dream of acknowledging my existence with a funeral.

Why did I have to dump the soup in his lap? What the hell was I thinking?

I glared down at my traitorous hands. The hands that had gotten me into this whole mess. If I could cut the offending things off, I would, but blood made me a bit squeamish. Just the thought of it made my stomach roll. Instead, I shoved the deplorable appendages into my armpits and paced the floor of my soon-to-be ex-room.

Ever since I'd arrived at the palace, no, ever since I'd seen the king's smug face as Angus, I had done nothing but act out. I wasn't that person. I was meek and accommodating.

Okay, that was a lie. I was only that way when I wanted to be, which usually was ninety-five percent of the time. It made life easier, especially in a world that didn't particularly care for my kind. Humans were tolerated at best, beaten and killed at worst.

Why in all the gods did I hate Balefire so? It's not like he did anything to me. I was the one who put a pie in his face, not the other way around. Of course, he would want retribution for such an act. The fact that he hadn't just asked for my head right then and there was concerning. Now that I knew that our just and fearsome king had a cruel side he was just hiding from the rest of the court, I should have tried to get fired immediately... or at least tried to run away.

The dragon. What about the dragon? I gulped and placed a hand over my throat. The kitchen staff said something about him having a dragon in the basement. Would he feed me to her? What was it they called her again?

Shirazan. Yes, that was it. I was for sure going to be her dinner now or worse. Maybe he'd boil me alive in the very soup I'd dumped into his lap.

I hugged myself as I paced faster. I couldn't handle pain, not that kind. I'd pass out and drown in it before it even got to the boiling point, I was sure of it.

No. There was only one thing I could do.

I had to run.

My mind set, I rushed to my wardrobe. I pulled out the measly possessions I owned and found my bag I'd come with at the bottom of the wardrobe. After shoving my clothes into the bag, I turned to the room. My eyes caught sight of myself in the mirror, and I gazed at the beautiful serving dress I'd been given. It wasn't technically mine. I shouldn't keep it. However...

Without thinking on it anymore, I started for my bedroom door. My hand reached for the handle, and at that very moment, a firm knock sounded. Startled, I jumped back from the door and clutched my bag to my chest.

They had come for me!

My breathing came faster now, and my heart pounded in my chest so hard that it sounded like a herd of stampeding hippogriffs. Twisting around, I sprinted across the room and to the open window. I poked my head out of the opening and glanced down at the ground. It was at least a forty-foot drop. I might survive, but I'd be hurt, possibly enough that I wouldn't even be able to escape.

The knocking became incessant. I chewed on my lower lip, trying to decide if scaling the palace walls was an option. Just when I was about to say fuck it and take my chances, Finch's voice called out.

"Ericka?" Finch paused before continuing when I didn't answer. "No one is going to hurt you. I promise. You are safe here." He muttered something that I didn't catch which didn't make me feel any safer despite his words. "Please, open the door, Ericka."

"Go away," I yelled out, one leg over the side of the window. My hesitation at the fall was what ruined it all. If I'd just taken the leap, gritted my teeth, and bore with it, then it would have all been over. I'd have been well on my way home and out of the wicked king's grasp. Unfortunately, that didn't happen.

The door to my bedroom burst open and startled me. That caused me to sway and start to lean out the window, releasing a squeak of terror from my lips. Finch was at my side in an instant. His hands wrapped around my waist and dragged me back into the room.

"No, let me go," I cried out and beat my fists against his chest. "Just let me go."

Finch took my beating until he had me several feet from the window, then his hands grasped mine.

"I will not let you kill yourself for this," he said firmly. "I cannot have that on my conscience. I have enough there already."

Tears burned my eyes as I shook in place, realizing my weak human body was useless against the fae before me. "Just kill me already and get it over with then. I won't be subjected to anything that would shame my family."

Finch sighed and rubbed his hands up and down my shoulders trying to calm me. It didn't work. Making a shushing sound, he brushed the tears from my face and tipped my chin up with his hand.

"No one is killing anyone today," he assured me.

"But I--"

Finch cut me off with a shake of his head and a smirk. "His Majesty doesn't kill people for accidents."

"But it wasn't an accident," I argued, though the smarter part of me wondered if I had lost all my brain cells by pointing it out. Something in Finch's expression told me it didn't matter. "You knew it wasn't, didn't you?"

Finch released me and took a step back. With a shrug, Finch glanced toward the door. "His Majesty can be a petulant child at times. He goaded you on purpose. His only mistake was thinking you wouldn't retaliate."

My terror morphed into anger. "I knew it!" I jerked a finger into the air. "I knew he was saying those horrid things just to piss me off."

"Yes, well, His Majesty doesn't always think things through. I had thought he was going to finally choose a mate, but it seems that it was all a ruse to torture you some more. Seems we were both disappointed tonight." Finch sighed and dragged a hand through his hair. "As it is, you will be punished." I opened my mouth to argue, my eyes darting to the open window once more. "Though it won't be death or anything that extreme, so no more climbing out the window." He narrowed his eyes at me, wagging his finger in my direction. "The last thing we need right now is servants plunging to their deaths. You have no idea how much paperwork that involves."

I huffed a laugh. I couldn't help it. He just sounded so dejected about having to fill out paperwork from me killing myself. Then against my will, my huff turned into a full-on belly laugh, one that Finch joined me in.

After a few moments, I wiped my eyes with the back of my hand and took large breaths as I calmed somewhat.

"So, what menial task does his majesty have lined up for me now?" I asked. "Wash all the windows in the palace? Clean out the stables? Polish his crowns?"

Finch winced as I named the items off. "Actually, you won't be doing any of those things. His Majesty wishes to punish you privately."

My stomach dropped down to my butt at the prospect of being punished privately. It could only mean something horrendous, something that no one in court would ever allow him to do and get away with it. The urgent need to escape came back in full force, and my eyes drifted over to the window once more.

"P... privately," I stuttered out, trying to figure out how I'd reach the window without Finch grabbing me first. "What do you mean, privately?"

Sighing, as if he were completely put out by the prospect of explaining the king's punishment to me, Finch lowered his tone, which in all honesty, made it only that much worse.

"For the humiliation you have bestowed upon him in front of his peers, he will bestow back to you tenfold."

Humiliation? What could that mean? Sure, I'd probably embarrassed him by dumping soup on him in front of his guests, but could he have really felt that strongly about it? I mean, it wasn't like it was his fault or anything. What could he possibly want me to do, or worse, do to me that would be humiliating?

I didn't consider myself a very proud human. It was hard to be proud of what you were when everyone around you was so extraordinary. I'd had my case of green jellies a time or two. Most of us humans just became used to the fact that we were nothing but ordinary, less than that in fact. There would always be a fae more beautiful, faster, better at anything we could do, and there was nothing we could do about it. So, my level of pride was already pretty low. I wasn't sure what the king thought he could do to make us even.

"What exactly does His Majesty want me to do?" I wrung my hands in front of me, my face the optimum point of concern as I waited Finch's reply.

Finch seemed to hesitate to tell me, but finally, with great reluctance, he took a deep breath.

"You made the mess, you clean it up," was all he said.

"That's it?" I frowned as I lifted my hands up at my sides and almost got excited for a moment. "I have to clean up the mess I made? Not that I'm looking a gift kelpie in the mouth, but I didn't expect such an easy task." I paused for a moment and hummed. "The king really doesn't know much about humans, does he? Because as far as humiliation, that's not even up there on the top ten list. I expected some boot licking or toilet cleaning at least."

Finch was abnormally quiet, allowing me to rant as I willed. When I finally stopped talking and turned to the door, he grabbed my arm.

"It's not that simple, Ericka."

I arched a brow. "It isn't?"

"No, it's not. You aren't just simply going to clean up the dining room mess. You have to clean the whole mess." He stared me down, clearly expecting me to catch on to what he was saying.

Growing impatient with all the cryptic crap, I threw up my hands and sighed.

"Just say it already. I might not be dumb, but I have no idea what you're talking about. What other mess would I clean up but the... dining room..." I trailed off, and my mouth slowly fell open. No. He couldn't mean... That's preposterous. Why on Tatiana's teat would the king want me to clean him up as well?

"You can't be serious." I shook my head as I backed away from him. "I can't do that. Doesn't he have concubines or something for that?"

"He wants you to do it," Finch pointed out with what looked like an apologetic smile. "I don't question His Majesty's commands, no matter how asinine they are." He muttered that more to himself than to me. Then he seemed to remember himself and give me a weak smile. "It won't be all that bad. Thousands of women, fae and human alike, would kill to have this honor."

I snorted, crossing my arms over my chest. "If it's such an honor, why is it my punishment?"

Finch gave a noncommittal shrug.

I thought about it for a moment. I had to help the king clean up. It couldn't be that hard. I mean, it would be just like the one time my father threw his back out. While mother ran the bakery, I helped him do everyday tasks, one of those being taking a bath. I could scrub his back... wash his luxurious royal hair... I gulped, my eyes widening as I realized what else His Majesty might make me wash.

Without warning, I sprinted toward the bedroom window and threw my leg over. I had just gotten my other leg over the window when Finch grabbed me around the waist.

"Oh, no, you don't."

"Ugh. No. I'd rather break my leg. Or my neck. Maybe even my hands. Then I couldn't do it. That's it!" I turned in Finch's arms and held my hands out. "Break them. Right now. Then you can tell the king I had an accident and can't do the job."

"Ericka." Finch gave me an exhausted smile. "If you don't do this job, he will find something else equally if not more humiliating for you. If I could give you some advice?"

I pouted and scuffed my foot on the floor. "Do I have a choice?"

"If you just suck it up, act absolutely boring, the king will become uninterested in you quite quickly. Then you can go about your life unhindered by all this extra... attention." Finch offered me an encouraging smile.

"Uninteresting. Boring. Yeah, I can do that." I talked myself up, staring down at the ground as Finch led me to the bedroom door. "I just have to steel myself. Don't react. Be like those robot things in grandfather's books. Yeah, I can be as dull as a rusty sword. The king will be begging me to go back to my real job. I can do this."

We stopped, and my eyes landed on the king's bedroom door. My heart leaped into my throat, and I shook my head violently.

"Nope. No. I can't." I spun around and tried to run the other direction, but Finch was there to stop me. I stared up at him with wide eyes and a panicked expression. "Finch, I can't. I've never seen a man naked outside of my father, let alone the king. This is... this is..." I clutched the labels of his jacket and sucked in quick breaths. "I think I'm going to pass out. I can't breathe. I can't..."

Finch placed a hand on my head, and a cooling sensation poured through me. All my fear and anxiety sank away until I was sure there was a dopey look on my face. I felt like I was flying, and my head was floating above the clouds and into the heavens. This was probably what those humans who snorted pixie dust felt like. I could understand the addiction. It was... niiiice.

"Ericka. Ericka." Finch snapped his fingers in front of my face. "I placed a calming charm on you. It'll help you get through this without incident." He arched a brow as a girlish giggle burst from my lips. "I hope I didn't give you too much."

"I'm good." I waved him off and turned toward the door. I gestured forward with a loud laugh. "Time to clean the royal ass!"

Finch groaned and mumbled, "Definitely too much."

I giggled once more and pushed through the door that was surprisingly open. I guess when you're the king, you didn't worry too much about others just walking into your room. Though, with how frightening he was to most people, I doubted anyone dared to come in unwelcome. I snickered. Probably worried about someone seeing him in his royal underpants. My heavy-lidded eyes scanned the bedroom of the beast of the fae court.

"Lame," I muttered as I realized his room was quite ordinary. Boring really. A four-poster bed sat in the middle of the room. Encased in dark blue, the only big difference between my bed and his was the size. It was massively huge, even for someone of his size, and it was ridiculous. Did he have orgies or something in here?

My cheeks warmed at the thought, and I quickly turned away from his bed. A wardrobe stood to one side of the bed, and a large desk was placed against the other wall. The desk was covered with papers and ink pens scattered in such disarray that I had to wonder if he had stopped in the middle of what he'd been doing. My gaze drifted from one side of the room to the other. Here was the king's room, but where was the king?

As if reading my thoughts, the king's distinct voice rumbled from an ajar door. "Finch? Is that you?"

The king was in the bathing chamber. Of course, he was. That's what I was there for. The anxiety charm was quickly evaporating into thin air at the thought. Was he nude already?

I walked toward the door, passing his laundry basket. Inside sat the clothing he'd been wearing at dinner. That answered that question. The king was no doubt nude.

"Finch?" Balefire called out once more and then after a small pause, "Human?"

I opened my mouth and shut it a few times before clearing my throat. "Uh, yeah. It's me. I mean, I'm here to help you bathe."

"Well, don't stand there all day," he hummed, and the sound of water sloshing made my spine stiffen. "Get on with it."

Licking my lips, I reached for the doorknob. As I turned it, I took a deep breath. He was just a man. A nude man. I pushed the door open to reveal the king lounging against the back of a steaming bathtub. Thankfully, his eyes were closed so I could get my fill of everything.

I took back everything I said before. He wasn't just a man. He was a fae man which made him unfairly gorgeous, especially for the personality that was attached to such a magnificent body.

His golden mane flowed over his shoulders and clung to his skin while water drops slid down his chest. The only thing I could be thankful for was that he was already in the bath, saving me from having to see the whole glorious package, pun intended, as it was being unwrapped.

One piercing blue eye cracked open, and a lazy smirked covered his lovely lips. Fuck. Get a handle on yourself, Ericka. He was an ass. A royal pain in the ass who was doing this to humiliate you. Don't get distracted by those rippling muscles. Though there were a lot of them. Fuck!

"Are you going to stand there and stare all day or are you going to come do your job?"

The rumbling growl of his voice did nothing for my libido. Nothing. Absolutely nothing. Okay, who was I kidding here? An ass he may be, but I now knew why all those women in the kitchen were cooing over him.

I cleared my throat again and moved toward the tub. There was a small stand next to the tub of golden metal shaped into vines and flowers. On top of it sat glass containers of what I could assume was shampoo and soap. A bright blue sponge sat next to the containers. Of course, he'd have one. They were expensive since you had to trade with the mermaids down in Leanan Bay, and they only came from the deepest part of the depths.

"Come now, human. This isn't too much for you, is it?" Balefire opened both of his eyes now, staring at me with a challenging smirk.

Boring. That's what Finch said. Be utterly boring.

I straightened my spine and kept my expression flat as I walked over to the stand and picked up the sponge.

"Would you like to wash first or your hair?" I asked with a monotone voice. To my delight, the king frowned at me, confusion furrowing his brows.

"You can wash my back first," he slowly said, still thrown off by my demeanor. Lifting up off the side of the tub, Balefire bared his back to me so I could wash it.

I walked around the tub and grabbed one of the containers of soap. Pouring a generous amount onto the sponge, it smelled of lilies and raspberries, I reached out and pressed the sponge to his back. I blanked my mind and scrubbed the sponge along his broad shoulders and back, trying my best not to notice the way the muscles rippled beneath the surface of his golden skin.

"Oh, lower," Balefire moaned slightly, and I paused, lifting the sponge. His head turned toward me and grunted. "Why'd you stop? Get to it. Lower."

I nodded, though he couldn't see me. I replaced the sponge on his back and scrubbed lower until the king let out a long, moaning sigh. Daaaamn. I was in trouble. It was harder to stay dull and uninterested in what was going on than I thought.

Stepping closer, I leaned over him as I moved the sponge up and over his shoulders. My other hand found its way onto his other shoulder, and I began to knead the muscles there with my palm. My mouth watered, and a low thrumming began in between my thighs.

That's when Balefire leaned back against the tub and forced my hands over his shoulders and onto his chest. His head pressed against my chest, and my breath caught. Not sure if this was some ploy to make me uncomfortable or not, I didn't say anything. I simply continued to wash him, moving in slow circles across his chest, pausing as the sponge caressed the heart shaped symbol over his left pec. He lifted his arms from the bath so I could sponge off each of them, something I did in great length, marveling at the strength in them.

When I was done cleaning his arms, I led the sponge back to his chest and had to push up on my tiptoes to get down to his abs. The water sloshed where the sponge plunged in and out of it as I scrubbed. My breath came in small pants now at the prospect of cleaning what was beneath the soapy water. The shadows and murky water made it hard to see what I was looking at, but what I could see made my cheeks heat.

Balefire's large hand caught my wrist, and I turned my head. Our faces were now only inches apart now. Our breath mingled, and our eyes locked. Bemusement and... maybe interest reflected out of the king's eyes. He couldn't be as affected as I was, could he?

Dropping my wrist suddenly, Balefire turned his head away from me. "I can finish it from here. Go back to your room."

All I could do was gape. I didn't know if he was serious or not. When he didn't say anything else or even acknowledge me, I dropped the sponge and straightened back up. Walking as fast as I could without running, I made for the door. I didn't stop until I was out of his room and safely back in mine.

Closing the door behind me, I sank against it with a heavy sigh. What the heck was that?

I didn't have time to think about what almost could have happened, because there was someone in my room.

A woman. Obviously fae, with long black hair that cascaded over her shoulders and pooled around her on my bed where she lounged. A slinky ink black dress clung to her curves and showed off her ample cleavage as she shifted to sit up on the bed. Horns the length of my forearm protruded from her forehead, and her ears were pointed as well as the majority of the teeth in her mouth. She flashed those sharp teeth in my direction as I moved away from the door.

"You've returned finally." Her emerald green eyes surveyed me with great interest before wrinkling her nose. "You're not much, are you?"

"Uh... I'm sorry?" My brows lifted. I didn't know why I was apologizing, she was the one who came into my room unannounced.

"As you should be." She shifted from the bed and slid to her feet in a move so smooth that it barely seemed like she had moved at all. Then she began to circle me, her fingertips pressed together in thought. "So, you're the human the whole castle is in such a fuss about? I don't see

what the big deal is. You're pretty, I suppose...
for a human."

I tried to follow her with my eyes, but I still
had to turn each time she moved to my back.
"Thank you?"

"But I cannot see what has the king so
intrigued." The creature stopped before me and
lifted a bit of my hair that had escaped from my
up-do. "He is mine, you know? Balefire might be
wasting his time playing with you, but don't
think that means anything. You're nothing.
Human trash that can easily be broken and
discarded." She grinned those sharp teeth at me
once more, dropping my hair as if it were
garbage.

Okay, now I was getting mad. I was tired and
emotionally drained from what just happened
with the king. I just wanted to collapse on my bed
and sleep. I didn't have time for some pissed-off
concubine.

"Who are you?" I asked as I barely held back
a snarl.

The woman seemed to sense it anyway.
Taking a step back, she waved her arms around
her in a flourishing sort of way. "Why, I am
Shirazan. Bringer of death and lover to the King
of the Spring Court."

Yep. Concubine.

"Look," I started with a tired sigh, "I don't
have any interest in the king outside of getting
him off my back. You can have him. I give you

my blessing. Now, please, leave. I want to go to bed."

I moved past her toward my wardrobe and opened it. When I saw that it was empty, I remembered I'd packed everything up. I searched for where I'd dropped my bag and found it by the foot of the bed. But when I moved for it, a hot ball of fire came barreling toward me. In a panic, I threw myself to the ground and covered my head with my arms.

Thank all the gods, I didn't get turned into a pile of cinders.

Shirazan laughed haughtily. "Next time you touch what is mine, I won't miss."

Then, as mysteriously as she appeared, she was gone. I lifted my head and quickly patted myself to make sure nothing had caught on fire. The scent of burning wasn't coming from me. My eyes drifted over to my bed where the center of it was burning brightly. As the fire began to spread, I jumped into action.

Running to the bathing chamber, I grabbed a nearby bucket and filled it with water. I rushed back to my room, the water sloshing over the sides the whole way, and dumped it on my bed. I did this four times before finally the fire was put out. I sighed in relief and sank to my knees.

There went my hope for getting to sleep any time soon.

Chapter 10

Balefire

I STAYED IN THE tub until the water cooled, but it did nothing for my heated blood. Finch had been right, the bastard, this had been a very bad idea. I should have never chose bathing me as Ericka's, no, the human's, punishment.

I groaned and collapsed on my bed, still naked, slightly wet, and not at all less turned on than I'd been when Ericka, I mean the human, had been here. I growled at my slip up again. Rubbing a hand down my face, I let my mind wander.

I'd never considered myself prejudiced. The humans were here living their lives, not trying to overthrow the fae or anything. They just existed. They hadn't given me a reason to care about them one way or the other. I certainly never paid two minds to them, certainly not enough to insult one right to their face.

Why then? Why had I purposely gone out of my way to say something nasty about the species when I knew Ericka was listening?

It brought up another issue as well. Why did I even care what she thought? Was this still all a game to put her in her place? Or was Finch right and it was something more?

I huffed a laugh, shaking my head as I stared up at the canopy of my bed. That's ridiculous. There wasn't anything remotely interesting about her. She wasn't overly beautiful. I'd seen prettier beings human and fae alike. Her hair was just a shade too muddy, and her eyes just a bit too dark... except when she was angry. Then they lit up like coal burning in a fire. They really were quite... mesmerizing.

Then there was the fact that she was too skinny for someone who spent their lives baking. Did she not eat her own creations? That was unsettling. I'd only tasted two of her foods, and both had been delicious. Insanely so. So, why was she trying to work in the palace where she'd fade into the background? Not when she could have her own shop somewhere and be the most sought after baker in the Spring Court. Maybe even all Elphame.

It didn't make much sense. Not much about her did, at least to me, especially the peculiar tingling feeling I got when I set her off. It wasn't a bad sensation, not in the least. The only feeling that had been better than pissing the human off had been the scent of her arousal.

I'd almost thought I'd drifted off during my bath, I was so shocked by the tangy sharp scent of it. What surprised me even more was the fact that my own body had reacted toward it. The moment it hit my nose, my cock had stiffened, painfully so.

The small sounds the human made while she was washing me made it even harder to resist pulling her into the bath with me. When her mouth ended up inches from mine, I almost gave into my need and ripped her clothing from her body. That crimson dress fit her like a glove, and the way it pushed her breasts up to the neckline would make any male's mouth who had eyes water at the sight.

I'd wanted to rip that dress right down the middle and pull her breasts into my hands, my mouth. I wanted to hear her whimper and beg me for more as I had her on top of me, underneath me.

I grunted as my hand found its way into my towel and wrapped around my aching cock. Hating myself for giving in to the temptation but knowing I wouldn't sleep otherwise, I kept the image of the human in my mind as I tugged my hand up and down my length.

A familiar sound filled my ears, the sound of magic and fire, but I ignored it, too far gone in my pleasure and shame. However, I couldn't continue to do so when a deep purr filled my ears and a hot hand trailed up my thigh.

"My, my, seems I was just in time, my king."

I didn't bother opening my eyes to see the owner behind the hand. I knew who it was. Only one person was brazen enough to come into my personal chambers without permission. Only one person, other than Finch, who wouldn't be punished for it.

Shirazan.

Gorgeous and dangerous as any fae female should be, she had a talent for knowing exactly what I wanted and when... but not tonight. Tonight, I wanted her gone.

"What do you want, Shirazan?" I tried my best to keep the annoyance out of my voice, she had a temper after all, but from the way she stiffened on top of me, I knew that I'd failed.

Still, after a moment, she relaxed once more. "Why, to please you, my king. As always." Her hand slid over mine, trying to take over where I had stopped.

"Not tonight." I grabbed her wrist and sat up, pushing her away as I swung my legs over the bed.

"Why not? You were already about to do it yourself. Why won't you let me take care of you?" I could hear the pout in Shirazan's words and could almost see those full lips of hers puffing up in my head.

I didn't want to look at her, not because she wasn't every fae man's dream. Quite the opposite.

Shirazan was tall and curvy in all the right places. Her breasts were blessed by the gods, and even in her aging years, they hadn't changed a bit. Dark hair laid against pale skin which I knew was as smooth as it looked. It tasted just as good as it looked.

However, she was harsh. Cold. Not in temperature but in temperament. Not like...

Dragging my sleeping pants on with a sigh, I glanced over my shoulder at Shirazan. The dress she wore was sheer and barely covered a thing even though it was long enough to brush her ankles. Tempting. Exceedingly tempting. But I couldn't make myself get excited for her. My mind and body were already set on someone else.

"I have a headache." I groaned internally at my pathetic excuse. What next? I'll be talking about my feelings? Wanting to share? Gods help me. "I mean, I have a headache of a political situation to fix. I don't have time for pleasure."

Shirazan frowned and cocked her head to the side. "I could always just..." She lifted her hand and fire appeared, dancing on her palm. "... squash the problem." She smiled viciously as her hand closed around the fire to snuff it out.

I almost smiled. "Not that kind of problem. Though, I wish it were." Gods did I. Not only did I have to worry about Ericka and the strange happenings between us, but I'd have to smooth things out with Nico and her father. I had no plans to take a wife, least of all one from the Fall court.

"This is about that human, isn't it?"

Shirazan's question threw me off, and for a moment, I didn't know what to say. The jealous gleam in her eyes told me that she knew exactly who she was talking about, and I knew that I had to tread carefully. While Shirazan might serve me, she could be a wild card at times. I'd always wondered when the day would come that she'd turn against me, but I didn't want it to be today.

Turning toward her, I crossed arms over my chest, using my size to show her I wasn't to be manipulated or questioned. "What I do with my property is my business. Do we need to reevaluate your position here in my kingdom?"

If my threat bothered her, Shirazan didn't show it. Her lips, colored a blood red, curved at the edges, not at all worried by my words. Her green eyes glinted though with malevolent intent.

"Of course not, my king."

I stepped toward her and tipped her chin up with my fingers. Our eyes locked, and the battle for dominance began underneath our gazes. Auras mingled, and we pushed against one another. The lashing out and testing boundaries was more so on her side than mine. I simply waited, guard up, but not attacking her back. I wouldn't lower myself to such an act.

Finally, after what felt like an eternity, Shirazan conceded. Her aura withdrew, and her hand reached up to clasp the one holding her chin.

"I owe allegiance to you alone, my king." Kissing my hand, she peered up at me from beneath her long lashes.

I didn't answer right away, searching for the lie. Fae as old as we were learned how to bend the truth until the lie became real. Such a true lie was almost impossible to detect and even harder to call one out on it. To claim a fae would lie was one of the rudest things one could do. Unable to hold back any longer, I released her with a growl.

"Do not take my indulgence of you for granted," I reminded her. "I might enjoy your company, but that does not mean you can push me."

"Of course not, my king." Shirazan fluttered her lashes at me, a demure expression on her face. It didn't suit her. Shirazan in her humanoid form was just as petty and dangerous as her dragon one. She may show me a face of complete surrender, but I knew better than to think underneath she wasn't rolling with anger. Spinning away from her, giving her my back, I waved a hand toward the door.

"You know your way out."

Her presence lingered for a moment longer before she was gone. Not for long I imagined. However, that was a problem for another day.

I placed my hands on the edges of my desk and leaned against it. My eyes stared down at the papers there but didn't comprehend what they were. When had I let my life become so complicated? Women at every turn pulling for my attention. Dignitaries thinking they could get in good with me by shoving their eligible and married daughters in my face. It was like no one believed I could do this job on my own. I had to have a queen by my side.

If only father was here.

Unfortunately, the previous king of the Spring Court was touring the human realm and helping them rebuild in ways they would never dream of. My father was a firm believer that if we rebuilt the human world, then the humans in our world would rush back like the vermin they were. His words not mine.

I knew better.

The humans have become content with their lives here. Sure, a few might go back, but many would rather stay where they knew they are safe. No one wanted to uproot their lives for a chance to live where their forefathers once did.

Did Ericka want to?

If given the chance, would she run away to the human realm and work as a baker there? She had the skills enough for it. All right, so I didn't really know what skills she had because I hadn't given her the chance to use them. I'd been too busy being petty and cruel to her. And for what? To get a rise from her? What was I, a hundred years old?

I scoffed at my own childishness. Crossing the room, I grabbed a pair of pants out of the wardrobe and pulled them on. Then, as I turned back to my bed, I paused. My head tilted to the door just seconds before a knock pounded on its surface.

With a long, drawn-out sigh, I walked across the room to the door and threw it open.

"What do you want now?" I said as I scowled at Finch.

Finch's gaze skimmed over my form, the agitation in my face, and bunched up shoulders. I tried to school my features, but he knew me too well. "Went well, did it?"

I wanted to punch the smile off his smug face. Instead, I shut the door in his face. Stomping back across the room, I flopped into my desk chair. I was too wound up to sleep now.

The door opened almost as soon as I closed it, and Finch strode into the room like he belonged there. He surely did more than anyone else in the palace. Besides Shirazan, he was one of the only ones who wouldn't get punished for it.

And Ericka.

I squeezed my eyes shut at the thought. I didn't know where it came from, but I knew it was true. If the human randomly came into my room after today, I didn't think... no, I knew I wouldn't punish her. Not in the way my citizens would expect anyway.

"You should know by now that doesn't work." Finch stood behind me, his arms crossed as he smirked down at me.

"Doesn't hurt to try," I said with a shrug. I lifted the first sheet of paper and skimmed the contents, pretending to be interested in the equalization of faeries versus pixies. "What do you want? I have work to do."

Finch leaned over my shoulder and picked the paper out of my hand. "I can see that. I can also tell Shirazan has been here."

"So?" I forced myself to not stiffen at his musing. "Your point? She comes by often. It's not like it's anything new." I shifted in my seat as I tried my best to misdirect his inquiries.

Finch snorted. "Only this time, your pet made a stop before coming to you."

This time I did stiffen. "What do you mean?" I glanced over my shoulder to meet his gaze.

Finch stood and adjusted the arms of his coat as he walked over to my full-length mirror while picking at his hair like someone who was going to meet his lover. I swung my chair around and stared at his back, waiting for him to explain. He would eventually, he always did but only in his own time. He might be my trusted adviser, but he was a right pain in the ass. When Finch seemed satisfied with his appearance, he twisted back to face me.

"Ericka had a visitor today," he began. "One that left her without a bed to sleep on and in dire need for a magical cleanup."

I found myself on my feet and halfway to the bedroom door before I knew what I was doing. Finch caught my arm, stopping me in place.

"No need to rush off. She's been relocated to the servants' wing for the time being, and I already have someone on the cleanup. I'll have her back in her own room by morning."

I relaxed and shook loose of Finch's hold. "Why didn't anyone alert me?"

Finch stared at me hard. "I'm telling you now."

"You should have told me the moment it happened." Irritation filled me and I bared my teeth at him.

"Frankly, I didn't think you'd care," Finch mused with an arched brow. He shifted his weight from one foot to the other, his hand on his hip, the same position he always took when he was about to lecture me. "You've showed no interest in Ericka other than to make her life hell. Why should I believe any different now? Not unless something happened? Something recently…"

I turned away from him, not trusting my expression. "Nothing of importance."

"If you say so, then it must be true." Finch hummed to himself. "But I do warn you to keep a close eye on your pet. Or you'll be finding yourself a new baker before the current one even has her chance at the stove."

Chapter 11

Ericka

THE ROOM FINCH SET me up with wasn't as nice as the one I'd had in the king's wing, but it wasn't exactly Boggsville quality. The mattress didn't sink in like a cloud, but it didn't exactly suck.

My spine would argue differently.

I groaned as I sat up and threw my legs over the side of the small cot in my new ten-by-ten room. While yes, I could walk from one side of the room to the other in under ten seconds, it was still bigger than my room back home.

Lifting my arms above my head, I stretched until my bones cracked and my skin tingled. I grunted and limped to the small bathing chamber off to the side to relieve myself and wash my face. I was tempted to duck my head under the cold water to wash away my lack of sleep and the scent of burned mattress that was still stuck up my nose. One look at the tub and flashes of last night came back to me full force.

Nope. No. Not gonna happen.

I just needed to clear my head. That was all. Just do something to get my mind off of him. It! Damn, I so didn't need this. I was barely surviving here as it was. I did not need an attraction to the king added to my plate.

I glanced down at the red dress from last night and grimaced. Step one to forget all this would be getting rid of this dress.

Untying the ribbon around my waist, I pulled the dress down my arms and dropped it to the ground. After kicking it to the side with my foot, I searched for my bag of belongings I'd brought over from my old room. I just needed to get back to the basics. Get back to what I came here to do.

Bake.

That's what I was good at, and I shouldn't be cleaning the floors, serving dinner to foreign dignitaries, or bathing the... king. My face warmed, and a weird sensation spread through me. I shook my head to clear it.

Right. Exactly.

I should be behind the scenes. Doing what I do best. Baking.

With my mind made up, I pulled a gray dress out of my bag and pulled it over my head. I searched for a piece of twine and twisted it around my hair so that it stayed up off my neck. My hair still stunk of the fire from, last night, but

I wasn't going near the bathtub, not now. Maybe not ever.

Shoving my feet into my shoes, I walked to the door, opened it, and poked my head out. It was quiet. Everyone else must still be asleep. I padded down the hallway and glanced out of a nearby window. The dawn hadn't even crested the horizon yet. I hadn't been up this early since I used to prep the bread for that day's baking.

With as much stealth as I could muster, I made my way to the kitchens. On the way, I passed a few guards rotating their shifts. We nodded in greeting and then went on our own way. No one from the kitchen staff was there when I arrived.

My fingers trailed along the center counter, and I picked up a stray knife and put it back where it belonged. Moving around the counter, I found an apron and tied it around my waist then moved on to the refrigerator. I withdrew a few items from inside and placed them on the counter, then I scrounged up a bowl and the flour before returning to the counter.

With a slight pep in my step and a song in my heart, I went about the same dance I had done all my life. A bit of milk here, flour there, a dash of salt, and my hands were deep in dough in a matter of minutes. I got lost in the movements of my hands, kneading and pulling the dough until it was pliable in my fingers.

I could get used to days like this. Getting up before dawn, having the kitchens all to myself for a change. No one demanding me to go here or do that.

And just like usual, when my fingers started to work, my mind began to work through its issues.

"It's not like I wanted to be attracted to him," I mumbled to myself as I grabbed a rolling pin. Scooping up a handful of flour, I rubbed it up and down the rolling pin. "Sure, he's attractive. He's the king of the blinking Spring Court. Why wouldn't he be attractive?" I pushed the pin into the dough, urging it to flatten beneath my ministrations.

"I mean, if he was a slaugh, then it would be a big deal. You know, dark and evil and ready to eat your eyeballs at a moment's notice, but he's not. He's light and good, and okay, he's a bit cranky, but it's not like he can help himself. He is a fae after all. They tend to get cranky in general." I busied myself laying the now thinned out dough into a round pan, pinching the edges as I went. "Not unless you're a sprite. Well, depends on the sprite, I guess. That one back at the village was a right bitch. She thinks I didn't--"

"You talk to yourself too, huh?"

My eyes jerked up. The head cook, Jasmine, stood in the doorway, hands on her generous hips and a small smile on her lips. That was something that she never had around me before.

With a nervous laugh, I picked up the bowl of filling I had set aside and tipped it into the pie crust. "It's a habit I picked up when I was a teen." A soft smile lifted my lips as the memory of how I started came to mind. "My parents were always busy with the shop, and being an only child with no friends, I had to find my own way to get my issues out." I chuckled and ducked my head as Jasmine stared at me. "Well, besides going on a mass murdering spree."

"We wouldn't want that." Jasmine came toward me, her eyes on the pan in front of me. "Sometimes this job can be lonely. This world too. Especially for humans."

"Yeah, I get that." I sighed and nodded.

"It's even worse when you work in the palace," she continued as her eyes lifted to mine. "I was the new girl once. I was one of the first actually." Jasmine paused to hand me the pan with the top of my pie crust and gave me a tight grin. "Did you know they used to have gnomes working the kitchens?"

"Really?" My eyes widened and my mouth dropped open a bit. "Gnomes?" I glanced around the room at all the high counters. "How did they even reach anything?"

Jasmine chuckled and rapped her knuckles on the countertop.

"Believe it or not everything in here is recent. This place originally looked like a miniature wonderland. First time I stepped in here, I thought I'd grown four feet." She grinned and shrugged. "Turns out the kitchen wasn't made for our size. Not like it is now."

"Oh," I mouthed, not sure what else to say. This woman had been one of the main people to make my life miserable here, and now, here she was talking to me like a normal person. It was weird. Awkward.

As Jasmine rounded the counter, I picked my pie up and walked it over to the oven. Sliding it onto the rack, I closed the door, stood, and pivoted on my heel. Jasmine stood inches from my face. A small startled sound escaped my lips, and my body froze.

"Uh, hey, did you need something? It's not quite time for everyone else to come down, but I could get started on my chores, I guess..." I trailed off and played with my hands, not sure why she was so close and staring at me so.

"No, no, don't worry about that. No more chores for you." Jasmine paused, her eyes boring into me. Her brows drew together as her lips twisted to the side. "I'm trying to figure you out, Ericka Burner. What's so special about you that has the king all flummoxed?"

"I don't know." I shrugged, my stomach churning with bumbleflies at the king's name. "Honestly, I'm as clueless as you are for why

Balefire has taken an interest in me." I grabbed my elbow and laughed nervously. "Sure, when we first met, I hit him in the face with a pie, and then there was the soup in his lap."

Jasmine's eyes widened at the edges, and I held my hands up as panic rose up.

"It was an accident, I swear. Well," I grimaced and shrugged, "one of them was."

Jasmine was silent for a whole minute, her blue skin so pale that I thought she might disappear into thin air. I stepped toward her and waved a hand in her face.

"Are you okay?"

"No, yeah." Jasmine shook her head and laughed before she stepped back from me. "I'm good. I'm fine. Did you really dump soup in the king's lap?"

"Yep." I popped the p at the end and inclined my head slightly. "I really did. In front of his guests too, did I mention that?"

"Wow."

"He deserved it," I pointed out with a smirk.

"Are you mental, or do you just have a death wish?"

I shrugged. "Maybe a little bit of both?"

"Well," Jasmine placed a hand on my shoulder and shook me a little bit, "whatever you're doing must be working because I've been instructed to let up on the torture. No more pot scrubbing, serving dinner, or cleaning the floors."

"Really?" I couldn't help the hope that filled my chest at the prospect of never having to clean another floor again. A bit wary of her sudden change of heart, I arched a brow and frowned. "What's the catch?"

Jasmine stepped back from me and turned to gather up the items I'd left on the counter. "No catch. King's orders. You are to do what you were hired to do." She held the door open as she smiled at me. "Bake."

Glee spread through my chest, and I found myself hopping from one foot to the other. The chance to actually get to bake for real and not just because I needed to blow off some steam was more appealing than riding bareback across the Elphame on a unicorn. Also, I couldn't forget the fact that I would no longer be doing the bulk of the grunt work. The only problem, the only thing that made my lips tip down in a frown, was the why.

Why now? What had I done to change the king's mind about making my life a living hell?

Flashes from last night made my face heat and my pulse jump. The slickness of the king's back, the feel of his skin beneath my hands, the strength of him. Gods, I'd never felt that way about anyone, and I hated the fae. Well, hate was a strong word, but I seriously disliked him. Balefire was a dick and a massive one at that. I shouldn't be having such naughty feelings for him. Not now. Especially, not when the situation that put me in his bathing chamber had been his fault.

If he hadn't been talking shit about humans, then I wouldn't have felt the need to dump soup in his lap. Then he wouldn't have had to punish me. That's right. It was all his fault. So, the weird attraction to him would be all on him as well. It wasn't me. I didn't want that. I certainly didn't want him.

Or did I?

"Are you okay?" Jasmine asked, concern crossing her face. "You look like you just went through every emotion there is in the span of a minute."

I swallowed thickly and pushed down the bile in my stomach. "Yeah, I'm good. Thank you for telling me." I hugged her, and she left her hands limp at her sides. "I really appreciate it. You've given me hope that I can actually make a home here."

"Well," Jasmine chuckled, patting me on the back, "let's start by not burning down the kitchen. Your pie is about to burn."

"Shit balls!" I released her and spun back around to the oven. Grabbing a towel, I opened the oven door and pulled the hot pan from the rack. I hurriedly placed it on the cooling rack set up to the side of the stove top and fanned the towel over it. I stared down at the rich golden crust and sighed in relief. It was okay. No charring.

Stepping up behind me, Jasmine peered over my shoulder. "What kind of pie is it anyway?"

"Actually," I grinned and grabbed the knife to cut into it, "it's a quiche. A one of a kind quiche. It's my mom's recipe that was passed down to her from my grandmother and her grandmother before that, and now she passed it to me." I grabbed a plate and scooped a slice of it onto it before turning to offer it to Jasmine. "She thought I might need something new and impressive to add to my arsenal. The palace is the top of the top as they say. If there was one place I needed to pull out all the stops, it would be here."

Jasmine took the plate from me curiously, and her nose dipped down to inhale the aroma. I knew exactly what she was smelling. The garlic, the gooey sharp scent of the cheese, and my favorite part, the bacon. Nothing could taste bad with bacon in it. At least, that was my motto.

I picked up a fork and handed it over to Jasmine who now seemed a bit more interested and less cautious of the plate in her hand. I watched with bated breath as she cut into the slice and then scooped up a heaping bite of my quiche. As she slipped it into her mouth, I let out a slow breath and closed my eyes. When she moaned, they snapped open as excitement billowed in me.

"Good?" I eagerly waited for her response, my eyes wide with anticipation.

"Good?" Her bright blue eyes lit up with delight. "No, this is great! Why has that idiot of a king been having you clean the floors when you should be making magic with a spatula?"

I shrugged and grinned. "Just lucky, I guess."

Chapter 12

Balefire

THE WORDS BLURRED ON the page before me. I rubbed my hand over my eyes to try to clear them. I'd been staring at the contracts for the banshee immigration for over three hours, and while I couldn't find any loopholes in it that would cause my people harm, I needed to be on my toes. I couldn't afford to mess this up. If the banshees moved into the western territory without any leash on their powers, then all hell would break loose. I couldn't have that.

My people were depending on me to make the right choice, and that didn't involve getting distracted by one human servant.

Ericka Burner. I couldn't get her out of my mind since the night she bathed me and we almost... Regardless, I didn't have time for distractions, which unfortunately included sleep. Every time I closed my eyes, I was there back in the tub with Ericka's hands on me... except we didn't stop at just almost kissing.

I sighed and dragged a hand over my face. Sleep was overrated. Who needed it? I'd gone four days now without barely a wink, and I was doing just fine.

Except the pounding in my temple that would not cease.

A banging on my office door made the pain in my head exponentially worse. I didn't get the chance to tell them to go away before Finch came strolling through the open door. I threw my head back against the back of my chair and closed my eyes.

"Go. Away." My voice came out as a raspy growl, which only made Finch chuckle.

"I see you're in a good mood." Finch's footsteps tapped across the floor as he approached me. He sat something down on the desk with the clank of dishes. A waft of something delicious wafted up from those dishes and tickled my nose.

I cracked an eye open to see the tray on the desk. Tiny red roses lined the edges of a white plate. On the plate was a slice of crust-covered meat pie. I knew from the scent of it that it would be as delectable as it smelled. My stomach growled.

Wasting no time, I grabbed the plate and fork and dove into the pie like a starving man. A look at the clock out of the side of my eye said I had every right to be. Eight in the morning. I'd been up all night again. This was breakfast again.

"You're still not sleeping." Finch sat on the edge of the desk, his eyes focused intently on me. "How long do you think you can keep going like this? We might live forever, but we do need the basics. You need to sleep eventually."

I grunted, not looking up from my plate.

Finch picked up the papers in front of me and leafed through them while I practically licked the crumbs off my plate. I ignored the arched brows and smirk my adviser sent my way before dropping the plate back onto the tray and picking up the bowl of steaming soup. This, I ate a bit slower. I was hungry not masochistic. Pain had never been my choice of poisons.

"So, the banshees are getting restless." Finch shuffled the pages before crossing his arms over his lap. "They are going to want an answer and soon."

I swallowed hard and dropped the bowl down on the tray harder than needed. A thin line splintered up the side of the bowl. I winced. I didn't mean to do that. With one hand I picked up the mug of coffee, the ceramic cup warming my hand almost to the point of pain. I ignored it and snatched the papers out of Finch's lap with the other hand.

"It'll get done. Just leave me be."

Finch stared hard at me, his head tilting to the side as he studied me. I hated when he did that. It was like he was trying to read my mind, not something he could actually do, but Finch knew me so well that he might as well have the ability. I busied myself drinking my coffee and not flinching under his unwavering stare.

Not wanting him to poke at something that didn't need to be poked at, I glanced around for something else to talk about because if I knew my adviser he wouldn't just leave unless I could prove I was fine. Which I wasn't. I felt like my eyeballs were going to fall out of my head, and my head would implode on itself at any moment. My gaze landed on the tray before me, and I licked my lips in remembrance of the delectable meat pie.

"Jasmine has really outdone herself today." I paused and furrowed my brow as I thought about it. "Actually, the last few days. You should tell Jasmine to keep up the good work." I scooped up my pen and tapped it on the table, focusing my attention to the contracts before me once more.

Finch snorted. "You could just tell her yourself. Actually, you should get out of here." He looked around the office and sniffed. "Things are starting to smell ripe in here. Have you opted out of bathing as well as sleeping?"

I stilled for a microsecond before scoffing, "No, of course not. You must be imagining things." I shifted in my seat and then growled at Finch. "Fine. It's been a few days. I just... I've been busy."

"Busy avoiding your problems." Chuckling to himself, Finch lifted his eyes to the ceiling. "Yes, I can see that."

I stood abruptly, my chair falling back so it clacked on the floor. "I am not avoiding. I'm trying to keep our kingdom safe. That requires time and sacrifices. So, what if I haven't slept in four days or bathed? It's all in the name of national security."

"You keep telling yourself that." Finch stood up as well and nodded with a sardonic grin. "But eventually no one will remember you're the king of the Spring Court if you smell like something that came out of the bog." He walked backward toward the door, his hands behind his back and no less than smugness on his face.

Sighing, I picked my chair up with a wave of my hand, letting the magic slide from my fingertips into the wood to lift it in the air and place it back underneath me. I thought I was getting off easy and went back to the pages before me.

"However..."

I leaned my head back against the chair and groaned. Of course, I wasn't that lucky. Finch always had to get the last word in. He could never leave well enough alone.

"What? What else could you possibly have to say now?"

Finch held the door in his hand and smirked in my direction.

"Those meals you've been eating. That food you've been scarfing down like it is going to be your last meal in the world..." To my annoyance, he paused for dramatic effect. "... wasn't made by Jasmine."

"Then who were they made by?" I asked, even though something inside of me knew what he was going to say before the worlds ever left his lips.

"They were made by that pesky little human you've been hiding from these last few days," he tut-tutted at me with a wag of his finger. "And if you want me to pass on your message... you'll just have to deliver it yourself."

I jumped to my feet again, but he was out the door faster than I could get to him, the prat. I banged my hands on the desk in frustration which made the lamp on it shake. With a scowl, I dragged both hands through my hair and then over my face before slumping back into my chair. Trying to push what Finch had said to the back of my mind, I picked up the banshee's contract once more and focused on the words.

After a few moments, my eyes drifted. To the tray. To the empty plate. I picked up the bowl of soul I'd devoured in seconds, and a small smile played on my lips. Catching myself, I put the bowl back down and shoved the tray further away from me... except I had put too much power behind the movement and knocked the tray and its contents to the ground. The glass shattered and scattered around the room.

With a sigh, I stood, walked around my desk, and knelt down beside the mess. I could have a servant come to clean it up, but it was my mess. I'd been the one out of control. Letting my emotions control me like some human. I snorted and rolled my eyes at my own actions.

Humans. Such weak and feeble minded creatures. So easily rendered useless by their pesky emotions. In all my six hundred plus years, I'd never let myself become so controlled by my own feelings... not until now.

If my father could see me now, he'd laugh at me. Call me a coward just like Finch had implied. I was hiding from a human. A child really. For what? Because my little game got turned around on me? Because I'd found myself attracted to the very one I was trying to teach a lesson.

Well, I supposed the joke was on me. I wanted her to learn her place, but in the process, I'd been the one to learn something. I wasn't as in control as I thought.

I picked up the glass pieces and chuckled. Maybe Finch was right. I did have some other reason for tormenting her.

Ericka Burner. Such an unimpressive human with a spitfire attitude. Brave to boot. She'd have to be for defying me so many times, or just stupid.

My mouth curved into a wide grin. No, not stupid. She didn't seem the type. I'd have gotten bored of her after the first day if she had been. Now, all I wanted to do was poke at her some more to see how she would react. Only this time, I didn't want her torment and fear.

I placed all the pieces of glass on the tray and stood from the ground. I started for the door without really giving much thought of it, then found myself walking down the hallway holding the tray like some servant. It was certainly something I'd never done before.

"Your Majesty." A wide-eyed red-headed human servant stopped before me, bowing deeply. Without lifting her head to meet my gaze, she held her arms out. "Please allow me to relieve you of that tray. I would be happy to take it to the kitchen for you."

I studied the woman for a moment, my head cocked to the side. So humble. So willing to help me in any way I needed without asking. Not like Ericka at all. If she had been the one to find me in the hallway, she'd likely turn on her heels and go in the opposite direction. Or knock the tray out of my hand.

I huffed a laugh at the thought.

"Your Majesty?" The servant's voice shook, and her eyes lifted just a fraction before they dropped again when I glanced down at her.

"No, thank you," I gruffly replied and pushed by her. "I want to take it myself."

I could feel the servant's eyes on my back as I walked down the hallway. I'd probably frightened her with my actions. I surprised myself that was for sure. Would Ericka be surprised? Grateful?

I found myself wanting to see her face right that instant. To see the way her mouth twisted into a sneer when I entered the kitchen, even as the rest of the servants bowed and scraped before me. It almost made me giddy, and my footsteps quickened.

The voices from the kitchen reached my ears before I pushed the revolving door open. They were talking about something that had happened in the village and laughing amongst themselves. Even Ericka was smiling from ear to ear, her hands buried in dough as she kneaded it to perfection.

No, she was perfection. That smile. It made her glow brighter than any fae I'd ever met. So... beautiful.

But it didn't last.

When her dark eyes met my blue ones and froze, the smile on her face dipped, and her hands paused their task. Her laughter was cut off at the quick, and the rest of them followed. Their eyes lifted to me briefly before dropping to the floor. Everyone stopped their tasks and bowed, as I expected, some on their knees and others simply at the waist.

Except for Ericka.

The anger I'd felt before at her defiance and disrespect didn't flare to life this time. No, pride filled my chest and my lips quirked up at the sides against my knowing.

Ericka's brows furrowed at my reaction, and behind those curious eyes, she built her defenses against me. She didn't trust me, not yet.

But she will.

I stepped further into the room and let the door fall closed behind me. The glasses on the tray before me clinked against one another, and Ericka's gaze dropped to it. I stopped beside the middle counter where she was gathered with the other workers.

Giving a small smile, I lifted and dropped my shoulders. "I seemed to have made quite a mess."

Ericka's attention flickered back up to my face, and her lips twisted in an incredulous smile.

"You mean, you threw a temper tantrum and broke them. Isn't that right, your majesty?" The condescension in her voice was thick and heavy.

The other servants stiffened around her, Jasmine, the head cook, lifted her gaze to Ericka, bumping her with her arm in warning, but it did nothing to dissuade the glower Ericka sent in my direction.

"What can I say?" With a hapless grin, I sat the tray on the counter and backed away. "I've been having a bad few days." I leveled her with a look that made her eyes finally drop back down to her dough, and her cheeks colored to a delightfully pretty pink.

Ah. She was still affected like me. No doubt thoughts of the night she bathed me had come rushing back to her mind. Something that I hadn't been able to chase away myself, even with the lack of sleep.

"Your Majesty?" Jasmine shuffled around the counter and bowed deeply, her hands clasped before her. "Please forgive Dahlia for not taking your tray for you. I will speak to her as soon as she has returned." The fear in her voice pulled at my chest which made my pride swell. Then my eyes slid over to Ericka, who was frowning at me. The feeling stopped.

Of course, she wouldn't be okay with me making others fear me. Humans. Such soft creatures. I almost sighed but caught myself.

"Dahlia is not in trouble, Jasmine." I waved her off, assuming the servant in the hallway had been the one she spoke of. "She offered to take the tray, and I declined." My lips curled up as I turned back to stare at Ericka. "I wanted to come down here and provide my appreciation for the recent change of pace. I have never tasted something so..." I placed my hands on the top of the counter and angled forward as I licked my lips. "... delectable."

Silence permeated the kitchen. The servants around us might as well not even have existed for all I cared. I only had eyes for the human in front of me. Ericka.

She studied me with an air of suspicion around her. Her head tilted to one side as she watched me. Did she see me as a predator playing nice to the prey? It wasn't far off. I did indeed plan to play with her, but this time, it wasn't with the intent to eat her.

Finch had been right all along. I wanted her. Her spirit. Her mouthiness. Even her disrespect of me and all things royal. Not to mention the way her breath caught, and her chest heaved as she bathed me. I'd never experienced such want for someone, and I'd had my fair chance at any woman in the kingdom.

Perhaps it was the challenge of it all. Maybe I would become bored as I finally broke her down and had her, but that was a risk I was willing to take. I just had to make her see that as well.

Ericka turned her eyes down and continued kneading the dough beneath her hands. When her voice finally came out, it wasn't hesitant but forceful and perhaps a bit amused. Something I could work with.

"I am glad Your Majesty appreciates my work. Just imagine you could have had it this way all along." Her lips, bow shaped and begging to be kissed, slid up into a smirk. "Had I not been scrubbing the floors and every other part of the castle and its inhabitants."

Her little jab at her recent punishment stirred my cock to life, and I couldn't help but tease her a bit more.

"Come now, it wasn't all bad. There were several places I could mention that needed a good rubbing down." Her eyes jerked up and met mine as her breath caught in her throat. "I have a few more that could use your delicate touch if you would be so inclined."

Her desire thickened the air, and I forced myself to keep control. The beast inside of me wanted nothing more than to grab her, throw her over my shoulder, and carry her out of the room to somewhere secluded. There, I would ravish her within an inch of her life and then some more.

To my surprise, as fast as the air filled with desire, it disappeared. My jaw tightened as her expression morphed into cool indifference.

"I'm sure Shirazan would be happy to help you with any of those hard to reach spots." She gestured to the dough in front of her. "As you can see, I have my hands full. Good day, Your Majesty."

It took me a second to realize she was dismissing me. Me. The king of the Spring Court! For a moment, blind rage filled my gaze, and the fae around me quaked. With Ericka completely ignoring me, even with her fellow servants quivering beside her, I took a deep breath and spun on my heel. Barreling out of the kitchen, I forced myself to walk slowly and not throw everything in sight.

That woman was going to be the death of me.

Chapter 13

Ericka

THE MOMENT BALEFIRE LEFT the kitchen it was as if a heavy weight had lifted. The presence of the king had gone, and with it, the servants began to move once more. Silently, they returned to their tasks, and while some of them gave me sideways glances, none of them dared to question me.

Except Jasmine.

Her aqua skin had paled as I confronted the king, and now, her pallor wasn't any better. She grabbed the tray Balefire had left on the counter and dumped the broken glass into the garbage bin. The loud clanking of dishes reverberated off the wall, making me flinch. I kept my eyes down and my hands busy as everyone wondered what the hell had just happened.

The heck if I knew.

The sight of Balefire after all this time hadn't lessened the sudden desire I'd begun to feel for him. That gorgeous face, those bright blue eyes, sparkling at me as he tried to get a rise out of me. He'd almost got one too.

His invitation to finish what we had started had done nothing short of light my body on fire. It had taken everything in me not to jump at his offer. While Balefire had done his best to avoid me, I'd done my darndest to push him from my mind.

However, once bitten and all that. I couldn't pretend not to be affected by his presence anymore. Even the mention of his name caused my body to react and my heart to race. I'd even caught myself smiling inappropriately when he was mentioned in passing.

This time, however, there were witnesses, and the thought of the fae and humans around me had been enough to keep me grounded. It hadn't been enough to keep me from smarting off though. I couldn't seem to help myself when it came to the king. My mouth ran away from me, and then next thing you know, I'm telling him to go shove it.

"Ericka," Jasmine stopped next to me, one hand on her hip and the other on the counter beside me. "What has gotten into you? Do you want him to send you back to the bog, or worse, behead you?'

I resisted the urge to roll my eyes. "He's not going to do either. Don't worry so much, Jasmine." I lifted a flour-covered hand to her face and patted it with a grin. "You'll get wrinkles on that beautiful face."

Batting my hand away with a scowl, Jasmine shook her head at me. "You are playing with fire, Ericka. The king might be entertained by your defiance right now but believe me he will get bored easily." She paused, then placed her hands on my shoulders and turned me. Those large cerulean eyes narrowed on me. "And now that he seems to not only want to punish you but bed you, you must be ever the more vigilant. Men, fae or human, only chase a woman for so long, and once they catch you, it's over."

"Then I best not let him catch me, eh?" I winked as I grinned at her, then twisted out of her grasp to continue my task of flattening the dough for the latest batch of pies. While the king had been pleased by my meals, I was still limited to pies and quiches. Jasmine offered to help me to expand on that. The soup had been one of the first new creations that had gone well.

When Balefire showed up and said he enjoyed my food, it took everything I had not to jump up and down in glee. Jasmine and the others had tasted my soup before they gave it to the king and had assured me it was great but hearing it from someone as critical like Balefire it warmed my heart.

If only my mother and father could see me now.

I let out a long sigh. My parents would never come here, not to see me working or just for a visit. Boggsville might not be the best place in Elphame, but it was their home and they didn't want anywhere near the palace or the king. If Balefire and his family had taught them anything, it was to keep your distance from the royal fae, and you'll live longer. I probably should have taken their warnings to heart, but I couldn't help it. I wanted to get out of Boggsville. I wanted to see the whole of Elphame not just the palace, though working for the king was a step in the right direction.

Now, to see the rest of the palace.

"So," I laid out the dough in the preprepped pan and picked up the bowl of raspberry filling, "where's a good place to have a picnic? I haven't been out of the palace since I got here. I think it's high time I got out of here."

Jasmine wrinkled her nose and took the bowl of filling from my hands. "Why would you want to do that?" She tipped the bowl and poured it into the pan. "It's much safer here. In the kitchen." Shifting the pan so the filling laid out evenly, Jasmine narrowed her eyes at her work. "Besides, there are many places that are off limits to servants, especially humans."

I held the dough that would be the top crust of the pie out and slowly laid it across the top of the pan. I worked on pinching the edges of the dough into the sides. "Safe or not, I can't just stay in my room or the kitchen forever. I need to get out. Breath fresh air. Doesn't the palace have a garden or something."

Jasmine didn't answer. Her eyes darted to that of Sybil and Daphne, two of the other servants who worked in the kitchen. Both fae had matching worried expressions on their brown faces, their beady brownie eyes pinched at the sides. Sybil lifted her shoulders at Jasmine and Daphne, crossed her arms, and jerked her head from side to side. Turning back to me with a sigh, Jasmine took the finished pie and handed it off to Sybil to put in the oven.

"There's a garden on the east wing of the palace," the nymph told me, "but normally, none of us would be allowed over there since it belongs to the king."

Her warning fell on deaf ears. All I heard was garden and east wing. The fact that it belonged to the king didn't matter to me. Who owned flowers? They were living things, not something you could just lock away and never share with others. Besides, the king needed a bit of disruption in his life, and I was just the human to do it.

"Well, I'm going to make myself a picnic and check out the garden." I moved to the cabinet and pulled down the things I would eat for my lunch. I glanced over my shoulder at the others staring at me with a mixture of horror and fascination. "You're welcome to join me."

Daphne turned away, going back to work on cutting vegetables for lunch. Jasmine frowned hard, her cerulean colored brows bunched so tight they looked attached to one another. The only one who seemed remotely interested in coming with me was Sybil.

The brownie shifted in place, her eyes darting to the others. They settled on Jasmine as if asking for permission to go. Jasmine lifted her shoulders and shrugged. Sybil's lips quirked up in a smile.

"I'm coming with you." Sybil bounced across the kitchen. She pulled out a basket from beneath the counter and piled the food I'd pulled out into it.

While Sybil and I worked on our own lunch, the others went back to working on the king's meal, every once in a while shooting us a worried but curious look. While it was our duty to help make the food for the palace, we were entitled to a lunch break ourselves. Besides, I'd already made the pie. My work was done.

"Are you sure you want to come with?" I whispered to Sybil out of the corner of my mouth. "I don't want to get you in trouble."

"Of course!" Sybil beamed, her dark eyes almost disappearing from the crinkling of her eyes. "I've never been to the garden in the east wing, and I never turn down a chance to explore."

"Your curiosity is going to get you both killed." Jasmine stopped cutting the bread in front of her and pointed the knife at us with a jut of her hips. "Ericka might have the king's eye, but you are just cannon fodder."

The grin on Sybil's face diminished slightly, but I wrapped an arm around the brownie and squeezed her to my side.

"Don't worry, I won't let the big bad fae king hurt you." I winked at her. "Besides, what's he going to do? Feed us to Shirazan for looking at some flowers? He's not that barbaric."

Sybil let out a shaky laugh as she exchanged a nervous look with Jasmine. After a few moments, she came to a decision. Sighing long and hard, she pushed a smile back onto her face.

"You're right. It'll be fine."

"Great!" I squeezed her one last time and released her. "Let's go. I'm starved."

After closing the top of the basket, I hauled our goods into my arms. As I brushed by Jasmine to go out the door, she caught my arm, so I twisted back to meet her gaze with a soft smile.

"Don't worry, we'll be fine. And if not," I lifted the lid of the basket and held up a container which held my very special mini quiches I'd saved for such an occasion, "I'll ply him with these and make my escape."

Jasmine pursed her lips before jerking her head shortly. She released my arm and turned back to her work. Relief filled my chest. Turning to Sybil, I grinned.

"Come on, the day is getting away from us."

After giving the room one last look, Sybil wrung her hands but followed me out of the kitchen. I should have felt bad for bringing her along with me. Just because I didn't seem to have a healthy sense of self-preservation didn't mean that I had to screw others up too. Then again, I didn't want to go alone, and Sybil seemed like she might be a great friend. I needed one of those right now.

"So," I began as we walked down the hallway toward the east wing, "how long have you been at the palace?"

Sybil dropped her hands, and her nerves seemed to fade away at my question. "I've always lived here."

"Really?" I arched my brows. "I didn't know any of the servants lasted that long."

"Why would you think that?" She giggled, covering her mouth with her hands.

I shrugged and frowned. "Everyone thinks the royals go through servants like sirens go through mates. I figured there wouldn't be any children growing up here."

"Not at all." Sybil grinned and shook her head. "The king and his family might have a temper, but most of us know how to keep our heads down and not make waves." She paused for a moment, her eyes moving around the hallway to nod and smile at other servants who passed by. Each of them greeted her by name and were happy to see her. Curious indeed. "My great-grandmother was one of the first families of brownies to come work for the royals. Before her, we weren't even allowed near the palace." Her lips dipped down for a second as she remembered. "If you think humans weren't wanted, brownies were just as disregarded as humans, maybe more so."

"Why's that?" I cocked my head to the side, curious to hear her story. I never knew the history of brownies. I thought they were just as well liked as any other fae. Apparently, I was wrong.

"Most fae think we are good for nothing more than cleaning up messes." Sybil scowled as she tossed her pitch-black hair over her shoulder. "That our brains don't work unless we have a rag in our hands." Her voice filled with annoyance as she continued. "No one ever thinks that we have actual thoughts and feelings. We don't all just want to scrub the toilets and floors. Some of us have other aspirations."

My ears perked up. "Like what? What do you like to do?"

Sybil stopped before a pair of glass double doors, not answering right away. The glass of the doors was painted in gorgeous roses and vines with thorns pointed out from the sides. Even though it was just a painting, the thorns were sharp enough that I feared that I'd prick my finger if I touched them.

Turning her head toward me, Sybil held her arm out and lifted the other arm as if she were stroking something against her arm. "I love to play the violin. If I had the choice, I would play across all of Elphame." A dreamy expression covered her face, her eyes looking far off at nothing at all. Then just as suddenly as she had begun, she dropped her hands and sighed, dejected. "But it won't happen, not in my lifetime. I'm nothing but a kitchen maid. No one would listen to me play the violin."

I placed my hand on her arm. Her dark eyes lifted to meet mine, and I smiled.

"No one should give up on their dreams. If you don't go for it, who will?" My smile broadened. "Do you think I got here because I listened to my parents who wanted me to stay safe and sound in the home they built? Where I would lead the exact same life as them?" Dropping my hand, I reached for the door handle and winked. "If I can change my future, so can you."

"Thanks, Ericka. I really appreciate it."

As I pulled the garden door open, I laughed. "Don't thank me yet. We both might not live through this adventure to see either of our dreams come true."

Chapter 14

Balefire

I TOSSED MY PEN down on my desk. Damn the banshees to the depths and back. Never again. Next time I'd let Finch handle the lot of them and save me a headache or two.

After two hours of negotiations and a few broken windows, I finally pulled an agreement out of the lot of them. The banshees would move into the western territory and would be allowed to hunt amongst the woods for wayward souls with the contingency that they leave the locals alone. Whether or not they obeyed the rules set for them...we'd know in the future.

But not today.

Today, I was free from listening to their wails and threats of war. I pushed my time sitting in the court off on Finch to handle and now had the next few hours free. Freedom that I would take full advantage of.

At first, my feet had directed me toward the kitchen. I didn't even realize where I'd gone until I stood before the swinging door. Thankfully, I stopped myself before going in.

Ericka had made herself clear. She didn't want to see me. She didn't want anything to do with me. And why should she? I'd been an utter beast to her and then tried to flip it on her like nothing had happened. It would take far more than a few compliments and an almost kiss to win her over, I could see that now.

But what? What did a human woman like Ericka enjoy?

"Bartholomew," I barked to my clergy, who sat nearby on the other side of my desk waiting for my command. The willowy druid stood at attention at my summons.

"Yes, Your Majesty?" His raspy voice made his words crackle like the wood of a fire. "How can I be of service?" He stood from the seat across from my desk, bending at the waist so that the bark color of his hair fell over his sharp angled face.

"If you were trying to woo a woman... say, a human woman..." I trailed off as Bartholomew lifted his head. Though he fought it, the druids lips twitched as if he wished to smile.

Knowing better, Bartholomew smoothed his expression out before answering. "Humans are quite different than fae. Fae women would swoon over a show of power, defeating one of her enemies, or perhaps a magical--"

"Thank you," I growled to cut him off, "but I did not ask for a lesson in our own species mating rituals."

"My apologies, Your Majesty." Bartholomew bowed so quick he almost knocked his head into the desk.

I waved my hand and made a rumbling scoff. Running a hand down my face, I gestured for Bartholomew to stand again.

"Humans, Bartholomew?"

With a pale face, Bartholomew lifted his head and twisted his lips to the side. "Humans are complex creatures."

A snort escaped me.

"Yes, it is true that they lack a certain civility and follow their baser instincts," Bartholomew quickly explained his expression becoming more strained at each word. "Their outlook on mating are far more..." He struggled for the word.

Sighing in annoyance, I grunted. "Stupid?"

Coughing a laugh, Bartholomew nodded. "In a word." He shuffled in place, placing one hand over the other before shifting again. "Each human has their own thoughts and feelings on love."

A barking laugh from me startled Batholomew into a step back.

"Love?" I scoffed. "There is no love but that of your family and even then, it is limited." Placing my hands on my desk, I leaned forward and met Batholomew's gaze, which he dropped to the ground instantly. "Tell me how to win her affections, love doesn't matter."

The druid flinched but didn't comment. Smart man.

"Even if..." He coughed into his fist and continued with hesitancy. "Perhaps, you might make your intentions clear to her... this human. It would go over better than her finding out your affections are not the same..."

I snarled in warning.

Bartholomew hiccupped. A tiny little squeaking sound that almost made me smile, but I forced a frown onto my lips.

"Well," I waved a hand at him, "get on with it."

Clearing his throat, the druid licked his lips. "Find out what she likes and give it to her. Chocolates. Trinkets. Flowers." He rubbed a hand over his mouth and turned his head to the side, muttering low enough I knew he didn't mean me to hear it. "Promises of love."

Ignoring the last words, I lifted my eyes to the ceiling in thought.

"She enjoys baking. Making things with her hands." I braced myself on the desk and glanced down. "I cannot give those things to her because she already has them."

"Then perhaps, something she doesn't have?"

I frowned. Something she doesn't have. What could that possibly be?

Seeing my confusion, the druid began to sigh but then caught himself. "Why doesn't his majesty think beyond material items? She's a human and one from the bog at that. There are bound to be some experiences she hasn't been exposed to yet." He rolled his hands in front of him as if to prompt me to figure out whatever kind of experience he was talking about.

"Spit it out already, you damn druid," I shouted, a growl in my chest and throat. The druid tensed and slapped his hands down to sides in response, and his fingers curled into the sides of his pants.

With wide eyes, the druid closed his gaping mouth before sputtering out, "The gardens."

"The gardens?" I cocked my head to the side and frowned, crossing my arms over my chest. "What about them?"

Bartholomew licked his lips. "They are closed to the general public. Servants included. Perhaps you might sway your lady by giving her a--"

"Personal tour. Yes," I mused, tapping my chin with my finger. "Brilliant idea. Yes, a tour of the gardens might just be what I need to get on the good side of the human."

Bartholomew stood there staring at me, smart enough to keep his mouth shut while I was musing out loud. Getting annoyed by the mere presence of him, I waved him off.

"You're dismissed."

Sagging in relief, Bartholomew bowed quickly before darting out the door.

Alone at last, I didn't waste any time. Leaving everything on my desk where it was, I headed for the door. First, I needed to make sure the garden was in the best shape for our tour. Perhaps, I would have Jasmine prepare a picnic to go along with our experience. With a little magic and a lot of luck, hopefully I would get Ericka into my bed and out of my head once and for all.

On a new quest, my feet hustled down the hallway and past several startled servants. I rounded the next corner, so close to my destination that I almost didn't see the pudgy council member headed directly toward me.

"Your majesty, I'm glad I ran into you." Randolf's round cheeks were red as if he had been running toward something himself.

Brows furrowing, I held my hand up. "Whatever it is, it'll just have to wait." I rushed past him before he could stop me, his voice caring behind me.

"But...but Your Majesty!"

Leaving him behind, I kept going until I found myself before the glass doors of our beloved gardens. The gardens had been in my family since the beginning of the Spring Court. The very first fae queen planted the first seed of magic here, and from it, grew a single rose. The magic from the rose then spread out across all of the land, covering fields, valleys, and hills with glorious foliage and only stopping once it hit the barrier of the other courts. We kept the original rose here, in the garden, locked away from any who would dare see to harm it, accidental or not.

Coming into the gardens without prior approval was a grave offense, one that not a fae in all of Elphame would dare to break. It was the perfect place to bring Ericka.

As I pushed the doors open, I took a deep breath of air. The air in here always seemed cleaner, more alive than anywhere else in Elphame. No doubt because of the lack of outside interference to the growth of the garden.

My booted feet sank into the plush green grass, and I knew I was home. Being the king of the Spring Court wasn't only a name. I was just as much a part of the garden as it was a part of me. The magic that ran through every vine, every branch ran through my very blood. Coming here always made my head clearer. My muscles loosened, and my skin tingled with the magic of the air. Sometimes I wondered why I ever left this place to begin with. I should remedy that.

I moved down the natural path, and my eyes skimmed the flowers in constant bloom. The reds and blues. The vibrant greens and startling yellows. Any color one could imagine was represented right here. Crystal trees sparkled beneath the natural light coming in from the glass dome above us. The branches reached for the sun as if they could touch it from down here.

I remembered climbing those trees when I was a young boy. I'd wanted to pick one of the many beautiful, burnt orange blooms to give to my mother. Unfortunately, while dazzling, those branches were also sharp and fragile as glass. I had crashed through the branches and onto the ground below. My mother, who had been singing to the rose, heard my cry of panic and rushed to my side.

I'd expected her to scoop me up into her arms and hold me tight, to tell me everything was going to be alright. But the moment she saw me there on the ground, her eyes darted to the tree. Outrage and dismay covered her face as she crooned to the tree, choosing to sooth it over her own child.

"You must never climb these trees again, Balefire," she'd chastised me as she led me out of the garden by my arm. I still remember the sting of her nails.

"But I only wanted to pick a flower for you," young me had cried as I held back my tears.

Scoffing at my words, my mother stopped us outside the garden doors. She knelt before me, her hands on my shoulder, and her grip hadn't lessened in the slightest.

"The garden is not a playground. You must have respect for where you came from." She gestured back to the garden beyond the doors. "This garden is us. It is everything, and if you hurt it, then you are hurting us. Do you understand?"

My young head nodded, tears sliding down my face. "I understand."

I sighed as the memory dissipated. My mother instilled my reverence for this place at a young age, and I learned that lesson well.

A giggle jerked my head to the side, and I cocked an ear toward the sound. Muffled voices came from further in the garden. Someone was here.

My jaw tightened, and my feet sped across the grass toward whoever had dared to trespass in my gardens. My chest felt tight and burned from rage. All thoughts of wooing Ericka vanished from my mind. The only thing in it now was the need for punishment and blood.

The sounds led me to turn down the path toward the center of the garden where I knew the rose that had created our world, and my need for violence roared to an all-time high. The laughter and chatter grew louder as my steps drew closer. One voice stood out from the chatter. It should have faltered my steps, but it didn't. All it did was cause my ire to grow further.

"Sybil!" the human I'd been so eager to share my bed with cried out. "You are so bad. I can't believe you did that."

My tattoos on my arm and chest burned as pushed through the final steps to the center. The clearing which marked the middle of the garden held the single rose encased by a glass cage which was then surrounded by a golden metal fence to keep all who would dare to touch it at bay. At the foot of the rose, sitting on a blanket covered in food just outside the fence was Ericka and who I could only assume was Sybil.

The brownie - Sybil - opened her smiling mouth to answer Ericka's comment, and it was she who saw me first. The light in her eyes diminished, and her voice went silent as her mouth hung open in utter horror. Enraptured by her fear, I let a growl rumble out of me. My eyes locked onto Ericka as she realized her friend was no longer paying attention to her. Slowly, Ericka's head turned, and the smile on her face dropped as her brows furrowed in confusion.

Sybil gained her bearings first. She scrambled to her feet, her head dropping down as she bent herself in half in an effort to appease me. It was in vain. Nothing could slake my need for violence. Ericka stood as well but slower. It was as if she treated me like some animal, thinking her glacial movements and held out hand would cause me to find another quarry.

"Your Majesty," Ericka's voice was low and steady, an attempt to be soothing, but it fell on deaf ears.

"You aren't allowed in here." The gravelly sound of my voice caused Sybil to flinch away, but Ericka didn't move an inch.

Ericka took a single step forward her hands still out in front of her. "We meant no disrespect."

"No disrespect. No disrespect?" A haughty laugh burst out of me and I had to fight back the magic trying to force its way to the surface. I couldn't lose control now. "Your very presence is an abomination on this place." My rage could not be contained any longer. My back arched and my arms flew out to my sides as a long, burning roar poured out of my throat. The walls of the garden shook, and Sybil, still bowing to me, shook in time with that roar. Even Ericka flinched, the abominable human who had no regard for her life or anyone else's, it seemed.

Good. She should fear me. Everyone should fear the raging beast inside of me. Well, now it had come out to play.

"Leave," I snarled as I took a heavy step forward. "Leave now!"

Sybil scurried away never once lifting her head to meet my gaze, but Ericka hesitated. It was enough to push me into action.

Before she could figure out what she had done wrong, I was on her. My hands, which had turned to claws, gripped her arms so tight that she squeaked in pain. I savored in her fear as the tinge of it filled the air. As I bared my teeth at her, I pulled her close until I could feel her rapid breath on my face.

"You think you can just go where you like? That you are invincible because I have a minute interest in you human?" I gripped her tighter, pulling her even closer. "You are not worthy of this place. You are... nothing."

She squeaked once more as she pushed against my hold on her. "I didn't. I don't. I didn't think I was doing anything wrong."

"Of course." I chuckled darkly. "Of course, you didn't think. You never do... but you will now." I released one arm and jerked her with me toward the door. "You will learn your place and learn it now."

Chapter 15

Ericka

I WAS IN TROUBLE. Big trouble. When I suggested we go to the garden, I didn't think that it would be a big deal. Also, when I mentioned it to the rest of the kitchen, none of them had told me how big of a no-no it would be. I certainly didn't expect the king himself to show up and blow his top off.

I winced at the grip Balefire had on my arm as he dragged me through the hallways. I'd never seen him this way. Sure, he was a major ass, but so far, he'd been all bark and no bite. Now, I wasn't so sure I was safe from that bite.

Now he seemed to be out of his mind with rage. While there was no outside difference to him, there was something different about him. His teeth seemed sharper than before, his gaze chilly. I feared what he might do like this.

"Where are you taking me?" I gasped, trying to keep my fear pushed down where it belonged.

However, it did nothing to keep my heart from racing and my palms from sweating. Had the king been holding my hand rather than my arm, I was sure he'd have felt it. Right now, I was less worried about embarrassment and more worried about where he was dragging me off to.

Balefire didn't answer my question, huffing a growl as we stomped through the castle. Servants and nobles scattered at the sight of us... or rather the sight of him. I cast helpless looks their way in the hope that one of them would step in to help me, but it was like I didn't even exist. Their eyes darted down, and their footsteps quickened in the opposite direction. Not that I could blame them. Had I been in their shoes, I probably would have done the same.

The king dragged me toward a part of the castle I'd never been before. It was darker here. Less populated and cold. A chill ran up my arms, and I wished I had my other arm to rub some warmth into them. When we started down a set of stairs, I'd had enough.

I dug my feet into the stone step and jerked with all my might, ripping my arm from his lethal grasp. Placing my hands on my hips, I glared at the king. I still had to tilt my head back because of his height which sadly made my glare slightly less effective.

"I'm not going anywhere until you tell me where you are taking me."

Balefire reached for me again, and I sidestepped back and then hopped back up a step.

"Don't touch me. I didn't know the garden was off limits. In like a punishable by death sort of way. You can't punish me for something I didn't know."

His jaw tightened, and his eyes narrowed as he studied me, searching for a lie.

I crossed my arms over my chest and lifted my chin. "I deserve to know where we are going."

After a moment, a dark rumble of laughter burst through his lips which made me jump in place. Eyeing him warily, I inched back another step, but before I could really run, his hand lashed out and grabbed me by the wrist. I struggled against his hold, but this time, he was ready for me.

"Let me go!"

"No," he barked, and he pulled me down the few steps I'd gone until we were nose to nose. "Knowing or not, it doesn't matter. You broke the law. Now, you must pay for it."

We started again down the stairs, but this time, I wasn't going to be a quiet and willing participant. I would not go to my death having never fought for my life. I just wouldn't.

"This is ridiculous," I argued at his back. "It's just a garden. What's so special about it? It's not like we were hurting anything."

Balefire grunted.

Pursing my lips in annoyance, I continued, "Besides, you can't expect all your servants to know right off the bat what is off limits and what is not. You need to have some kind of orientation or a sign." I hummed as my brows furrowed. "Yes, a big sign with large letters." I used my other hand to pretend I was holding a sign up. "Do not enter, or the king will have a hissy fit."

The king stopped so abruptly that I banged into his back so hard that my nose stung from hitting it. With one hand, I rubbed the end of it as Balefire spun around, leveling those bright blue eyes on me.

"You do not even know the word self-preservation, do you?" he roared. "You just talk and talk, thinking that you can get away with anything just because I--"

"Just because you what?" I arched a brow, slowly lowering my hand.

"Never mind." Balefire shook his head, his golden locks swaying with the movement. "Never mind." With that, he spun back around and stomped even more forcefully down the stairs. The stairwell became even darker the further down we went. The only light came from the sparse torches sticking out of the walls.

"Why don't you have electricity down here? It seems kind of dangerous to be climbing so many stairs in the dark," I mused. My fear had mostly disappeared, mainly because he didn't seem as angry as before. I had that effect on people. Some loved me to death or hated me on sight. I was happy to say that I had more admirers than haters, though that was more for my current condition than back home, where I was too busy to make much of a single friend.

"She likes it this way," was the only answer Balefire grunted out to me.

"She who?" I lifted my hand to my face, looking from side to side as if the dark stairwell would give me some answers.

"My dragon."

For a moment, my eyes dipped down to his lower half a warm heat spreading over my cheeks. Why would he call his... thing a she? Then it dawned on me. Oh. An actual dragon. I was worse than a siren in heat! At the thought of Shirazan, nervousness filled me, and I jerked my arm once more.

"No way, no. I'm not going to where that crazy bitch lives. She already tried to kill me once."

Angling his head back to peer at me from the side of his eye, Balefire sneered, "With good reason I'm sure."

"Ha! Good reason?" I placed my free hand on my chest and glared at his back. "My very existence was enough to piss her off. I'm not going anywhere near her after having actually done something wrong."

"So, you admit you were wrong? That's surprising." I could hear the smile in his voice even if I couldn't see it.

"Now, wait just a second. I never said I was wrong. I still stand by my ignorance." The moment the words came out of my mouth, I wished I could take them back. There was no way he wasn't going to twist that beyond hell and back.

To my surprise he didn't do anything but grunt as we stopped before a door. Releasing my arm, he searched the dark nook next to the door for something. When he found it, a key, he slid the metal into the door and turned the lock. Pushing the wooden door open, he gestured for me to enter.

"Not gonna happen." I shook my head, my eyes wide and my mouth hanging open. "You're gonna have to kill me."

Light twinkled in his eyes as he reached for me, and I wasn't sure if it was a good look or a bad one, but I knew if I went in that room, I wasn't coming back out until I was extra crispy. Balefire's fingers curled around my arm and pulled me forward until our chests pressed together. Had I not been in fear for my life, I'd have swooned after I smacked him upside the head of course.

"What do you think you are doing?" I gasped as I pressed my hands to his chest, trying with all my might to separate us.

"You think death would be a better alternative than your punishment?" Balefire questioned with a tilt of his head. "Do you really not care for your life?"

I stared at him, mouth agape for a moment before snapping it shut. "Of course, I do! But I'd rather die a swift death than be burned alive by your crazy mistress. After all, I did break a rather important rule. Don't you think I deserve an important death? One that requires full attendance of the court and... and..." My eyes darted around as I tried to delay the inevitable. "And Finch. Finch should be there. He is your adviser, isn't he?"

Balefire's eyebrows furrowed and then his eyes narrowed on me. "What of Finch?"

As I saw that I had caught his attention, I kept going, letting my mouth get away with me.

"Finch is far sounder of mind than you are, your majesty." I gave a mock bow as I backed away from him. "It's no wonder you can tie your own shoes, let alone make a decision without Finch by your side."

Teeth gritted and jaw tightened, Balefire wagged a finger at me. "You would do well to hold your tongue, human."

"Oh, so we're back to human, are we?" I laughed haughtily. "I should have known better than to think that speech this morning was anything other than one of your little ploys." I crossed my arms over my chest and raked my eyes over him. "No doubt you were just itching for a reason to toss me to your dragon. Did you even like my food?"

"Do you dare accuse me of lying?" He took a large step toward me, and I shuffled backward until my back hits the door frame and he loomed before me.

Swallowing down my rising fear, I stared up into his eyes and lifted my chin in defiance. "If the pixie fits."

Balefire's hand shot out, and his thick fingers wrapped around my neck. My feet lifted off the ground, and I wiggled like a worm as I tried to break the hold of his grip. He wasn't squeezing so much as holding me up, but still, it wasn't exactly comfortable.

Unfortunately, for all my poking and provoking, he didn't take the bait to give me a public execution where I might have had a chance to talk my way out of it. Instead, he drew us into the wide-open room with a stone walkway, which surrounded a large hole in the floor. The ceiling was open so that the sky could be seen, and the afternoon light poured in to give the room a rosy coloring. Balefire moved toward the edge of the stone walkway and held me out above the hole. My feet dangled in the air, and tears burned my eyes. My nails scratched and clawed at the hand holding me, but it didn't seem to affect him in the least.

I didn't want to die like this. I didn't want to die at all. But me and my big mouth. I couldn't just leave well enough alone. I had to make things worse. Everyone was right. I did have a death wish. I was surprised I'd lasted this long without ending up dead or worse. Now, I was going to get that wish.

A low growl caused the walls to rumble around us, and I struggled to take in breaths. My fear caused my lungs to forget how to work. I fought to pull in breaths of air but couldn't find my breath. My eyes flew open and locked with the cerulean blue gaze of the king of the Spring court. I took gasping breaths and got out one word.

"P... please."

Balefire's hard glare softened for a moment, but then the sound of beating wings interrupted whatever connection we had. His face hardened once more, and I released his hand, letting my arms fall out at my sides. If I was going to die, then let it be with dignity. I closed my eyes with a resigned smile, counting down every heartbeat until he released me into oblivion.

Oblivion never came. Wind moved around me, tickling my hair, and then the hand on my neck released me. A small cry released from my mouth as I expected to be plunged into the dragon's lair. Instead, my feet hit the stone walkway, and I settled back down onto my feet. My eyes fluttered open, my vision blurry as my lungs relearned how to breathe once more.

Standing before me with a bewildered frown on his face, Balefire dropped his arm down to his side. He glanced between the pit and me for a few moments before something in his expression changed. Then, Balefire turned on his heels and left me there in the rose-colored tower. When he was gone, my knees crumbled underneath me, and I collapsed to the floor.

I'd almost died. I was a hair's breadth away from dying, I'd even accepted it, but he'd just stopped. Why? More importantly, why the hell did I think that I could get away with anything? I was a human servant for God's sake and a lowly kitchen one at that. Why would the king want anything to do with me other than eat my food?

I sat on the stone walkway and let the coolness of it beneath my hands ground me for several minutes. I didn't move from that spot until there was another ground-shaking growl that reminded me exactly where I was hanging out at. Scrambling to my feet, I darted for the door and slammed it shut behind me. I hurried up the stairs, taking them two and three at a time. All to get away from the death that might still be waiting for me.

My lungs burned by the time I reached the top of the tower stairs, but still, I did not stop. I walked in a hurried fashion all the way across the castle and back down to the kitchens where I threw the swinging door open. Everyone stopped what they were doing when they saw me.

Sybil who sat in the corner of the room with a tear-streaked face, blinked up at me.

"Ericka! You're alive!" She rushed across the room and gathered me up into her arms, holding me tightly in a hug. I hugged her back with just as much enthusiasm, laughing through my tears of joy.

"Yes, it seems I am for now."

"You are one lucky human." Sybil giggled and leaned away from me, then hugging me close once more. "I swear you have twelve lives, just like a jackal."

"More like a sire," Jasmine huffed, and my eyes flew to the other fae. She wiped her hands on a cloth and came around the counter. "You could sing your way out of anything, it seems."

"Not everything." I stepped away from Sybil and walked slowly toward Jasmine. "I almost didn't this time."

"But you're here, aren't you?" The head cook placed her hands on my arms and studied me. "That's all that matters."

I sighed and shook my head as I moved away from her. "Why didn't you tell me the gardens were forbidden-forbidden? You only said no one but the royals usually go there. I would never have gone had I known."

Jasmine dipped her head in shame. "I really thought you would be okay."

"Why would you think that?" I gaped at her as the other servants looked on at us.

Lifting a shoulder, Jasmine's lips ticked up for a moment before dropping. "You have the attention of the king, and no one besides that wretched dragon ever has gotten his interest the way you have."

I was dumbfounded at her reasoning. Throwing her hands away from me, I turned around the room.

"You are all ridiculous," I said. "He doesn't care about me. He was more than happy to feed me to his pet dragon just for being in the gardens. That alone should prove that I'm just a kitchen maid to him. Nothing more."

A small woman who hadn't said much the entire time I'd worked there, but I recalled her name was Margie stepped forward. She twisted her red curls in between her fingers her amber eyes burning with interest. "But you lived."

"What?" I eyed her with confusion.

She stepped forward and released her hair, her expression more determined than before. "You claim you are nothing special, but by standing here right now you are more than special. You faced the ire of the king and lived. That alone makes your exceptional."

"Well, I'd rather the dragon have eaten me," I scoffed.

"No, you wouldn't." Margie told me sharply as her eyes slashed into me. "No one would want that fate. Least of all you." Before I could ask her what she meant, she spun on her heel and stalked from the room.

I stared after her for a moment and then glanced back toward Sybil and Jasmine. "What did I do?"

It was Daphne who came forward this time. Her brown face flushed and her beady eyes bright with anger.

"You were being your usual self," she explained. "Instead of worrying about the king, why don't you worry about those who work and live with you? Like Margie." She threw an arm toward the door Margie had left through. "Her brother was eaten by Shirazan a few years ago."

"Oh," I breathed, and then my eyes widened. "Oh! I didn't know. I should go find her."

"No." Jasmine shook her head and took me by the arm, leading me to the counter where they were prepping dinner. "She just needs a bit of time, and you need a distraction."

"I don't know." I eyed the cutting board, and the beginnings of a stew before me. "I've never been very good at stews. Besides, after my life just flashed before my eyes, all I want to do is hide in my room until the king forgets all about me."

"Now that's a sure fire way to make sure you do die next time." Daphne snickered, bumping my shoulder as she passed by. "If anything, you should be making sure he remembers you and why."

"But... I..."

"She's right you know." Jasmine shot a look to Daphne and then back to me. "If I know anything about our king and men, it is that they need to be reminded why you are important, especially when they want to strangle you for being you."

My lips twitched. "It sounds like you have had some experience in that area."

Jasmine side-eyed me and then winked. "I haven't been head cook for three hundred years without picking up a thing or two."

We laughed and chattered as we worked together. I wasn't sure about making the king remember why he kept me alive, but I did know that working side by side with others who loved to cook as much as I did was exactly what I needed.

Chapter 16

Balefire

THE CLANG OF CLASHING swords filled the air of the training room. The pressure of the metal against my own blade sang up my arm, my biceps pulsating with the effort of the parry. Sweat trickled down my neck as I put myself through a vigorous workout.

Master Simone stood across from me. His brow was relaxed with no trace of the same fatigue I was feeling. Then again, the elder elven fae trained five hours a day every day for the last eight hundred years. It would only make sense he wouldn't be as winded.

"You are out of practice, Your Majesty," the lilted tone of his voice mocked me as he put me through my paces.

I growled as I pushed him off and circled to his right. I lunged for him, and he easily dodged, smacking me on the backside as he went.

Jumping at the contact, I narrowed my eyes on him.

"I'm running a kingdom, I hardly have time to sleep, let alone swordplay."

Master Simone angled his head to the side, his silvery grey hair bound up in a braid fell to the side as his matching eyes surveyed me.

"But you found time today? Tell me," he feigned left and I fell for it, earning myself another smack to the back of my thigh, "what has you troubled?"

I scoffed and swirled the hilt of my sword in my hand before taking up a defensive stance. "Are you my therapist now? I thought only humans did that."

"There is no shame in clearing one's mind and heart," Master Simone explained while he lazily waited for my next move. "One cannot expect to win battles against their foes if they cannot win against themselves."

"You know how much I hate riddles. Just say what you mean," I huffed and swung my sword at where he stood only to miss. I spun around searching for the elder fae, only to end up with a foot in my back and my face in the dirt of the training yard.

Grunting, I quickly rolled to the side just in time to dodge the sword that was now where I had once laid. Now flat on my back, I threw my legs down with as much momentum as I could and lifted the rest of my body off the ground.

Master Simone clucked his tongue at me, shaking his head. "You never were the most astute of my students. I fear you were too interested in what your father was doing than learning how to hone your mind and body."

"Well, I can tell you, my mind is perfectly fine."

We clashed swords once more. With something to prove, I put more strength behind my movements, trying to knock him off balance. The sly devil figured out what I was doing and slid to the side in the blink of an eye. I couldn't pull back my sword fast enough, and all that power I put into my swing had me falling toward the ground. I shifted my foot and caught myself before I ate dirt. I twisted my upper half round just as Master Simone's sword came down at me. Catching his sword with mine, I grunted as my knee buckled under me. I struggled to keep myself from falling completely while the cheeky git seemed completely unaffected.

"You cannot hide it from me," Simone continued as if were having afternoon tea and not a battle of wills and strength. "You may believe your mind is fine, but I can see the images swirling behind your eyes. Even now." Those grey eyes squinted, peering into mine as if he could see directly into my soul. "A figure clouds your mind. A woman. She's right there in your eyes. Why don't you tell me about her?"

Ericka.

The very thought of her spurred me into motion. I shoved onto my feet once more with a roar, throwing Master Simone back as I swung at him over and over again. He blocked and parried my strikes with ease which only enraged me more. My attacks became more violent, more erratic as I tried to erase the image of Ericka from my mind.

The human had become more trouble than she was worth. Every time I thought I had her figured out, she did something foolish, like trespassing in the garden. Then when I sought to punish her for her actions, she would turn it on me again. I never planned on feeding her to the dragon, I only wanted to scare her into submission. Show her that her actions had consequences, and she needed to think more sanely if she wished to survive in the palace.

However, that had not gone as planned either.

When I had her hanging there above the dragon's lair, I expected her to beg me for her life. To promise me anything, anything if I would only let her live. When she cried please, I thought I had finally broken through to her. She only needed one final push to get her to fully submit to me.

I was an imbecile. As quickly as she had pleaded for her life, she changed. As if she had figured something out and was resigned to die with dignity. I could applaud her that. I myself would never beg for my life. My stubbornness wouldn't allow it, and neither would hers apparently.

Still, when she simply stopped her clawing at my hand and went limp in my grasp, I'd almost dropped her. She had looked so peaceful, her face free of worry even with tears streaking down her face. Ericka really was an enigma, one I hoped to unravel soon before my mind went first.

Jumping away from Master Simone for a moment to get my bearings, I tracked his movements and looked for an opening. His left hip shifted, and I narrowly dodged the pointed end of the blunt sword coming my way. It wouldn't kill me, but it would hurt like a bitch. Iron was the only true enemy of the fae. Even the smallest quantity could kill us if used in the right way.

We parried back and forth until I grew confident in my movements. Maybe I grew too confident. I swung at him only for the bastard to disappear, and then my feet were out from under me and his sword was at my neck. Glaring up at the smirking fae, I scrubbed my hand over my mouth and grunted.

"Perhaps, I could use a bit more training."

"Perhaps." Master Simone sheathed his sword and offered me a hand.

I took it gratefully, and he pulled me to my feet. As I sheathed my own sword, I walked to the side of the training room where a servant waited with a towel and a glass of water. With a grateful nod, I took the towel and wiped the sweat from my brow and neck.

"The problem is that every time I think I'm getting two steps forward, I end up five steps back," I mused. "I just don't know what to do."

Master Simone approached us and took the other glass of water off the tray. He closed his eyes and mumbled a prayer before downing the glass in one gulp. With a loud sigh of pleasure, he sat the glass back on the tray and turned to me.

"If there is anything I know in this life, it is fighting and women."

I snorted which earned me a chastising frown. "My apologies, do go on."

"Whatever you know about women, especially human women, forget about it." I listened to him speak as I sipped from my glass. Master Simone was anything if not sincere. "You cannot win her heart with all your posturing and elaborate schemes."

I opened my mouth to argue, but Master Simone beat me to it. "A simple kitchen cook is not the same as a duchess." I didn't even bother asking how he knew exactly who I was talking about. It seemed I wasn't as secretive with my feelings as I thought. "The way to her heart will be the way to yours."

I threw my head back and groaned in frustration. "Plain words, Master Simone. Please. No more riddles."

Huffing in amusement, Master Simone poked my chest right above my heart. "Be yourself." With a slight grin, he turned and walked away.

I stared at his back for some time with a frown. Be myself? How the hell was that going to impress her? No, he must be wrong. I'd already screwed this up royally when I lost my temper at the gardens. I highly doubted I was going to be able to get her to talk to me, let alone fall for me.

As I walked back to my room to bath, my mind ran over the last few weeks events, from bringing Ericka to the castle to my mental torture of her. I groaned at my own foolishness. I was doomed. There wasn't a god in the heavens that could fix what I'd broken. I'd be surprised if she hadn't run for the bog by now.

My nose crinkled at the thought. Perhaps not.

Stopping at my bedroom door, I pushed it open and tossed my towel to the side. It landed on my desk chair with a thump. Stripping as I went, I made my way to the bathing chamber and prepared the bath. Normally, I would have a servant do it, but there was a simplicity in preparing someone's own bath, as if it made the bath that much more soothing. That was something else Master Simone taught me, the crazy riddle spouting bastard.

Sinking into the hot water, I released a long heavy breath. All my muscles relaxed as I sank further into the tub. There was nothing like a bath to soothe the mind and the body. I let my eyes flutter close as my mind wandered.

There had to be some truth in Master Simone's words. However, I'd never been myself when alone, let alone around someone like Ericka. How exactly was I supposed to know what myself was? If there was anything that defined me, it would be the garden, but I'd already ruined that. Maybe I could do something else. Something that she liked instead?

That was a new problem. What did Ericka like? I didn't know much about the woman. Being from Boggsville, she must have a high constitution. I couldn't imagine living somewhere that stunk as bad as it did. The one time we toured through the little town near the bog had been enough for me. I'd avoided it ever since, sending an emissary to gather any taxes or complaints instead.

So, besides her upbringing, she loved to cook. Pies and quiches seemed to be her specialty though it seems that she had picked up a few more dishes since moving here. There had to be something in that I could use. Perhaps...

"Well, well, lookie what we have here," a sultry voice crooned from the doorway.

I cracked an eye open and turned it that way. Shirazan leaned against the door frame, her black dress clinging to her body like a second skin.

"What do you want, Shirazan?" I sighed and closed my eyes once more. I didn't have the energy for this right now. Maybe if I wished hard enough, she would disappear. I peeked through my eyelids.

Nope. She was still there. In fact, with a cackle-like giggle that ground in my ears like rock salt, she sashayed to the side of the tub.

"Do I need a reason to see my lover?" Her long bony fingers reached out and trailed through my damp hair.

"I'm tired." I resisted the urge to pull back. Instead, I grasped her wrist with my hand. "Maybe another time."

"It's been weeks, Your Majesty." Her lower lip poked out in a pout, and she shoved her breasts closer to me as if that would change my mind. "I thought you might have forgotten about me." Shirazan paused, and something wicked flashed behind her eyes. "Or perhaps you found a new plaything. That human cook?"

My eyes flipped completely open. My grip on her wrist tightened for a moment as I pushed myself up and out of the tub, bringing her up with me.

"Leave the human out of this. She's of no concern of yours."

Shirazan's sharp green eyes fluttered down my body, a caress that I used to find appealing but now made me nauseous. With a dreamy sigh, her eyes moved back up to settle on mine.

"You made her my business when you brought her to my lair." She flashed a fang-toothed smile.

"That was a mistake."

Pushing her back, I stepped out of the tub and reached for a new towel. As I released her, I wrapped it around my waist and brushed past her to the bedroom. Ignoring the feel of her eyes on my back, I flopped down into a nearby chair without a care that I was getting it wet in the process.

Shirazan surveyed me with appreciate eyes as she swayed toward me, her hips moving in a tantalizing dance. "The only mistake was not dropping the wretched creature into it. I could have used a snack. I'm absolutely famished." She ended by dropping her knees before me, her hands on my thighs.

The urge to push her away was strong, but I knew the dragon well. If I denied her, she would claim it to be because of Ericka and use that as an excuse to take out her competition. Any fae woman would do the same, and I couldn't do a damn thing about it, king or not. Against my better judgment, I allowed my legs to fall further apart and her hands to glide up the expansion of my thighs, her face all too close to my groin.

"See...?" she beamed, her tongue sneaking out to lick her lips. "I knew you still wanted me."

I grunted and turned my eyes to the side. "What I want is a good meal and sleep. You are just convenient."

"A convenience?" A flash of annoyance crossed her features, before she smoothed her face out into a seductive pout. "Little ol' me? I'm flattered. I thought I'd made it quite difficult for you to catch me."

"But I did catch you." I leaned forward and grabbed the hand that had reached beneath my towel mere seconds away from grasping my very uninterested member. "Now, I'm bored."

"I see," Shirazan murmured slowly, pushing up to her knees so our lips were millimeters apart. "Just one more kiss then? Then I'll be on my way."

Sighing in frustration, I grabbed the back of her head and pulled her mouth to mine. No matter what she said, I knew this wasn't the end.

Chapter 17

Ericka

I SPENT THE REST of the afternoon in the kitchen with the other servants. It took my mind off of what had almost happened to me. At least, until I arrived back at my room.

Now, alone, all of it came crashing back.

My knees wobbled, and I sank to the floor. My back against my bedroom door, I grabbed my chest as racking sobs burst through. I'd almost died. I could have died. Why did Balefire stop?

There was so much about the king I didn't understand. So much about the fae world I didn't know. I'd lived here my whole life, and still, I couldn't comprehend the violence and bloodshed the fae seemed to thrive on.

When I was a little girl, I once saw a fight break out in the marketplace. Two fae went at each other like it was just a normal Tuesday. The humans rushed to their homes and closed the doors and windows, hiding their children. The fae stood around them in a circle cheering or jeering them on. My mother had ushered me back into the bakery, but I snuck over to the big glass window that usually displayed that day's goods. My little face peeked above the shelf, watching with astonishment as they tore each other apart. When they were done and only one was left being clapped on the back by his peers, my mother caught me and sent me to bed without dinner.

I didn't sleep well for a week after that.

One would think that I would be used to the mayhem that was my life. Sometimes I wished I'd never come to the castle. I wished to be back at my parents' bakery without a friend in the world but safe. I'd been in more danger since living at the palace than I ever had back home.

Sure, it was boring there, and it smelled like the stinky underside of a troll's armpit, but it was familiar. It was home.

Here, everything was politics and watching what you said and did. I could only truly be myself while I was cooking, and even then, I had to be careful. The fae that worked with me were nice, normal even, but they were still fae. They still had the ability to turn rabid at the smallest slight.

If I was truthful, I didn't want to be here anymore. I wanted to go home. I needed to go home. But to do that, I would have to talk to the king, and that wasn't something I wanted to do ever again.

My teeth ground, angry at me for my weakness. Look at me! I was blubbering on the ground like some pathetic creature. I was everything the fae thought humans to be. They didn't believe us equal or worthy of being respected or protected. And why? Because a king threw temper tantrums like a child?

I couldn't let him treat me this way and get away with it. I wouldn't. If I wanted to go home, I would, and there wasn't a damn thing he could do about it.

He could kill you.

He already tried and failed.

But you can't leave without telling him.

Why not? He didn't ask me if I wanted to be fed to a dragon.

Still, you have to at least say goodbye.

I chewed my lower lip as I mulled over the thought. I was angry with Balefire, of course. Who wouldn't be? But my mother taught me manners, and those manners demanded that I tell him of my intentions. If I tried to run away without telling him that I was leaving, I could cause issues for not only myself but for those in the kitchen. While I hated him the most right now, I couldn't do that to them.

I wiped my tears roughly off my face and stood. Going to my bathing chamber, I poured some water into my hands and washed my face.

No reason to let him see that I'd been crying. Not when I was leaving. I had some dignity.

Glancing in the mirror, I nodded at my appearance. Not perfect, but it would do.

I turned from the mirror and brushed my hands over my hair and dress. The dress was partly covered in flour, but I didn't want to change. If I did, then I might have time to talk myself out of this, and I couldn't do that. I needed to go home, and I had to talk to Balefire.

With a renewed determination, I marched to my bedroom door and flung it open. Finch was on the other side.

"Woah!" Finch held his hands up in front of him, his eyes wide. "Going out?"

Flabbergasted, I fumbled for an answer. "Uh, yeah. I was going to, uh, talk to the king."

"Why would you want to do that?" Finch's brows furrowed.

"Because," I huffed as I pushed past him and into the hallway, "I want to go home."

"Home?" Finch chased after me, his long legs easily keeping up with my short ones. "Why would you want to do that? You just got here."

I didn't answer him, my eyes forward and focused on getting to Balefire's room. However, Finch grabbed my shoulder, stopping and turning me.

"What did he do now?" he groaned.

To avoid his gaze, I stared hard at the wall. I couldn't tell him what happened. He'd just stop me from seeing Balefire, and I couldn't let that happen.

"Nothing," I mumbled and crossed my arms over my chest. "I just wanted to discuss... kitchen things. Yeah. We need new pots in the kitchen." I lifted my chin, meeting his gaze and almost daring him to call me out in a lie.

"You know, there's a form for that. I'm sure Jasmine could fill it out for you." Finch frowned. "You don't need to go to the king for that."

I held back my huff of annoyance and shrugged off his hand. "I know, but I want to ask him in person. If I wait for the form to be filled out and then given to him, it will take weeks to get them, and we need them now."

Finch hurried after me as I tried to get away. "What's wrong with the ones you have now? They worked perfectly fine at lunch."

I scrambled for a reason but came up with nothing. Stopping in place, I placed my hands on my hips and glared at him.

"Look, I need to talk to the king," I pleaded. "Why do you need to make a big production of this? Can't I just want to talk to him."

Watching me curiously for a moment, a slow sly smile slid up his face. "Oooh, I see. You want to 'talk' to the king. I see his plan to get into your good graces has worked. I hope he at least apologized for his mistreatment of you."

"If you could call it that," I scoffed and rolled my eyes.

Finch chuckled. "Our king has a hard time expressing himself, I'm sure he meant well. Obviously, it did something for you, or you wouldn't be so keen on speaking to him now."

Oh, it did something for me alright. Made me want to run for the bog. Something I never thought I'd ever say in my life. Playing along as the lovesick human, I fluttered my lashes up at him and pretended to hide a blush.

"I just want to get to know him is all. Can I go now? I don't want to miss him before he goes to dinner."

Finch waved me on with a nod. "Go on. The gods know he needs some happiness in his life." I spun on my heel and practically sprinted away as Finch's voice followed me. "Good luck!"

I waved a hand behind me, all the while clenching my jaw so hard, I thought it might break. When I arrived at Balefire's door, my nerves reared their ugly head. My heart pounded in my chest, and my hands became clammy. I'd been determined to talk to him, but now that I was at his door, I wasn't sure exactly what I was going to say.

Sorry, you're such a dick, but I can't take it anymore?

Make your own damn food, I'm out?

No, I had to say something that wouldn't make him come after me. Maybe I got word from my mother that my father is sick? On his deathbed? And I had to go see him before he died? Yes, that's it. A family emergency. He would have no reason to worry or try and come after me.

My hand touched the door handle, and I prepared to open the door. A giggle stopped me. It was muffled and faint, but I heard it. I held onto the door handle and pressed my cheek against the door my ear straining to hear behind the wood.

A low moan followed my distinctive smacking filled my ears. Someone was in there with him. Who? Shirazan?

Rage rolled through me, and before I knew what I was doing, I threw the door open and found exactly what I thought before me.

Balefire sat in a chair, clad only in a towel. His hair and skin were still damp from his bath, but what really caught my attention was the scantily dressed fae pressed between his thighs. Her hands tangled in his hair, and her lips attached to his. Balefire had one hand on the back of her head, but nothing else was touching her, almost as if he didn't want to be kissing her, but he didn't precisely push her away. Guess he couldn't have wanted her gone that bad.

A small gasp escaped my throat, and Balefire's eyes flew open. They locked with mine, and in the next instant, he threw Shirazan out of his lap and stood. Unfortunately, the towel around his waist did not stay tied and fluttered to the ground uselessly. My eyes darted down to his groin, my cheeks heating.

"Ericka," Balefire growled out, his voice husky with desire, "what are you doing here?" He didn't even seem to notice that he wasn't wearing his towel anymore.

Shirazan sure did though. She eased to her feet and then wrapped her arms around Balefire's shoulders and waist.

"Oh, look," she growled, but her tone wasn't full of desire. It was full of venom. "It's the human. What do you want, human? We're busy."

My eyes jerked between them, from her hands on him to his face. He seemed annoyed, but he didn't push Shirazan off him nor did he give me any explanation. So, it must be me.

My mouth dry, I licked my lips and shook my head. "Never mind. I shouldn't have come here." I twisted around and rushed down the hall, not bothering to close the door behind me.

I couldn't believe what an idiot I'd been. Sure, I was coming to tell him I was leaving but a small part of me hoped he'd beg me to stay, to apologize for what happened. But he wouldn't have done either. I was just another human for him to play with and then discard when he was done with me. Which based on how I'd almost died today, my expiration date was closing in soon.

Chapter 18

Balefire

"I THOUGHT SHE'D NEVER leave." Shirazan purred as her fingernails scraped along my shoulders and chest. "Now, where were we?" The hand on my chest moved down, trailing over my abs and reaching for my--

"Stop." I grabbed her wrist and flung her away. Reaching down, I picked up the towel and threw it in the laundry basket. Then I turned my back on her, went to the wardrobe, and threw the doors open. Not caring what I grabbed, I pulled on a pair of black pants and a light blue button-down shirt. My eyes flicked up to Shirazan as she huffed and then smoothed her hands over her hair, a playful smile on her lips.

"Oh, so we're playing that game today. I can play along." Her hands moved over her neck and down her body, cupping her breasts in her hands as she moaned. With a shrug of her shoulder, one strap of her dress and then the other fell off her shoulders. A slight shimmy and the entire dress fell to the ground, leaving her bare to the world.

Normally, at the sight of such beauty, my cock would harden, and I would waste no time burying myself inside of her before sending her on her way, sated and pacified for a time. Not this time. The very sight of her nude form made me think of Ericka. The long expansion of Shirazan's legs compared to Ericka's no less impressive but shorter ones. The slight swell of her hips had nothing on Ericka's curvy ones. While Shirazan forced seduction and sex into her every movement, Ericka caused my blood to rush and my cock to come to attention just from being covered from head to toe in flour. That human didn't have a sexy bone in her body, and yet she made me want her, nonetheless.

"Shirazan," I sneered, my lip quirking up in a scowl, "put your clothes back on. You're embarrassing yourself."

When I turned my back on her to find my shoes, a seething presence pushed against my back. I had not made her happy. However, giving her more attention would only cause myself more trouble, so I shoved my feet into my boots and made for the door.

Shirazan had reclothed herself by then and caught my arm. "You are rejecting me? Me! No one rejects me and gets away with it." Her nails dug into my arm, and I didn't give her the satisfaction in knowing she'd made me bleed.

Leaning in until our faces were close together, I met her glare with a smile. "You'll get over it. Now, get out of my room, and don't let me see you causing havoc. We have enough going on without you on a rampage."

Leaving Shirazan raging in my wake, I threw open the bedroom door and searched the hallway. No sign of Ericka. With quickening steps, I made my way to Ericka's bedroom door and Leaned in to listen for any sign that she was in there. She'd been so upset when she saw me with that dragon bitch. I knew I should have sent Shirazan away when I had the chance, but I was worried about what she would do if I denied her. The dragon was playing nice because she thought she had me wrapped around her finger. I worried about what she might do now that I finally cast her aside.

Finally.

While it had been fun for a time, a heavy weight had been on my shoulders for a while now, even before I met Ericka. Part of me wanted a reason to get rid of the dragon, and now that I had one, I needed to be sure that Shirazan didn't take it away. I needed Ericka more than I knew.

If she would even talk to me now.

I sighed, raised my fist, and knocked.

"Ericka," I called out, hoping to hear her sweet voice through the door, even if it was in anger. When she didn't answer, I knocked once more. Still nothing.

When I turned the doorknob, I found it unlocked. I pushed the door open and stepped inside, closing the door behind me. I could tell right away she wasn't there. Her room was dark, her bed made up, and no sound came from the bathing chamber.

Where could she have gone?

I searched the room for some kind of answer but found nothing. With regret in my heart, I stepped back into the hallway. Perhaps she went to the kitchens. I could try there first and if she wasn't there... well, I wasn't sure where she would have gone. It wasn't like I followed her around all day.

But, before I could make my way to the kitchens, Finch appeared in the hallway distressed. His hair was frazzled, and his cheeks flushed. He grabbed my shoulders the moment he saw me, and relief flooded his eyes.

"Your Majesty, thank the gods I found you. We have to hurry." He rushed away from me and down the hall toward the throne room. I ran after him. Did it have something to do with Ericka? I could only pray that it had nothing to do with Shirazan.

"What is it? What's wrong?"

"The banshees." Finch glanced over his shoulder at me. "They're claiming that they were cheated and are demanding payment for the slight. I tried to explain the contract to them but they--"

A screeching sound pierced my ears. Finch and I clamped our hands over them to fight off the power of the wail. Somewhere in the palace, glass shattered, and screams erupted.

Damn. This was just what I needed right now.

"Come on." I smacked Finch on the arm. "Let's go deal with them before they pull the whole place down on top of us.

Finch and I ran through the corridors, passing servants and nobles scrambling to get as far away from the screaming as possible. While I wanted nothing more than to search for Ericka, to apologize, or even to explain, I had to deal with this problem first. Ericka, unfortunately, would have to wait.

As we rushed to the throne room, I wished for the power of teleportation. Of all the gifts that I had been given, that was one that had been left out. Things would be a lot simpler if I could just appear where I needed to be, consequences be damned.

When we arrived at the throne room, we found the place in a fit of chaos. Bodies lay strewn across the marble floors with blood leaking from their ears. A dozen palace guards had the six banshees surrounded, their spears and swords pointed in their direction. Thankfully, they had earplugs in their ears, or they would be on the ground as well. It was a precaution we always had when banshees entered the castle. If I'd known they'd arrived, I'd have put some in as well.

Banshees were temperamental creatures made of darkness and sound. Some say they are the lost souls of women who have had their hearts broken, that their pain had grown too great, and in a fit of despair, they screamed until their hearts shattered. What was left were barely functioning beasts with long white hair and sharpened teeth and nails. The color of their irises were turned white as their eyeballs with only little black pupils left to see by. Their ratty grey and black cloaks covered their pale bodies which I knew were bony and malnourished. While they were one of us, they were nothing more than rapid animals seeking their next victim.

I should never have let them stay in my court, but the other courts would have seen me as prejudiced against the dark fae had I not tried. After this though, this pointless bloodshed, there was no way I could let them live.

"You sorry excuse for a fae cheated us," the leader of the banshees, Hester, hissed as she pointed her thin and jagged finger in my direction. The blackness of her claws seemed to absorb all the light around us.

Stepping to the edge of the circle of banshees, I crossed my arms over my chest and leveled a glower at them. "I did no such thing. You signed a contract, one that you were supposed to read. If you did not understand all the terms of your deal, then that is by no ways my fault."

"You think you are so smart with your big words and prettily worded lies." Hester shook her head, her ragged hair jerking around her face. "But no one makes fools of us." She held her arms out around her and her sisters, her eyes boring daggers at me. "We will eat your entrails after we make your men bleed. We will wear your teeth as a necklace around our necks. You will rue the day you--"

"Blah, blah, yes, yes, I will pay." I waved her off with an annoyed sigh. Finch stood at my side looking just as annoyed as me but slightly more worried. The banshees could be a problem if they got away, but I wouldn't make the same mistake twice.

"You dare interrupt me!" Hester cried out, and then threw her head back and let out a long wail.

I gripped my ears and fell to my knees, my pain and irritation morphing into rage. A nearby guard handed me a pair of earbuds, and as I shoved them into place, I stood.

"You have broken your contract by attacking the locals where you were, graciously I might add, given sanctuary," I growled as my fingers curled into fists. "As per the contract, you have forfeited your life." I lifted my hand before me, aiming in the direction of the six banshees. "A sentence that will be delivered, now."

I funneled my rage into my chest. From there, my magic swelled and trailed up my arm. Fire burst from my hand and engulfed the six banshees. Their cries of pain rang out through the room, dulled to my plugged ears. No one came to their aid. No one even batted an eye at their suffering. They had broken the law and had to pay for it. Such was the way of our kind.

Except for Ericka.

She had broken many a law, and still she lived. Some might call me insane. Enamored. And maybe I was. If I was under anyone's spell, it would be Ericka's, and I planned to tell her that very thing once I found her. If I found her. Those were my thoughts as I slumped onto my throne, the servants cleaning up what remained of the banshees.

"When did things get so complicated, Finch?"

Finch glanced away from the clean up to me. Arching a brow, he smirked. "In what way, Your Majesty?"

"I remember the days where the worst of my worries was what noble emissary from the other courts were plotting a royal wedding." I waved a hand at the wreckage. "Now, I'm dealing with banshee outbreaks, Shirazan's jealousy, and..."

"And a certain human who seems as crazy about you as you are about her." Finch stared off at the servants working with a secretive look on his face.

"What?" I leaned to the side to look at him. "What are you talking about?"

"Oh, she didn't tell you?" Finch's gaze turned back to me amusement twinkling in his eyes. "I ran into Ericka earlier, and she was determined to talk to you. I swore by now you two would have been entangled in sheets when I came to find you." He frowned. "Why weren't you? Did you mess it up again?"

"When don't I when it comes to that woman?" I grunted before I shook my head with an ironic laugh.

"What happened? Didn't you talk to her?" Finch shifted completely to face me now, real worry etching his features.

"Oh, she came to see me alright." I sighed and rubbed a hand over my face. "Talk? Not so much. And as far as enamored with me goes, if you count wanting to poison my food counts as love, then she has it in spades."

"I think I'm missing something here."

"Quite a few things actually," I murmured and shifted in my seat. "The most recent being she saw me with Shirazan."

"She saw you two?" Finch's bows rose and then they narrowed as he glared at me. "I hope you mean, she saw you kicking that hot-headed back stabbing dragon to the trenches and not what I think you mean."

With a depressing groan, I sank further into my throne. "Not so much."

"Balefire!" Finch cried out, causing the servants and guards around us to glance our way in alarm. My advisor wisely lowered his voice then. "You were not fucking that harpy while you are in love with Ericka."

I held my hands up and pushed him out of my personal space. "First of all, who is king here? Secondly, of course not. And thirdly, I never said I was in love with her."

Finch snorted, shaking his head. "You may be king, but you are still so young it kills me." With a huff of annoyance, he asked, "Well, where is she now? You might have enough time to fix it before she completely shuts you out."

I lifted a shoulder and frowned. "Hell, if I know."

Chapter 19

Ericka

GETTING MY BAGS PACKED wasn't a problem. I'd never unpacked from the first time I tried to run. It was as simple as grabbing the bag from the bottom of my wardrobe and then fleeing down the hallway before Balefire could follow after me.

My breathing heavy, I made my way to the kitchen. When I pushed the revolving door open, my heart sank. They were cleaning up from preparing dinner and singing a song together as they worked, something that I had enjoyed greatly after I was finally allowed to be with them. This was something else that Balefire had taken from me.

As I pushed back the tears that threatened to fall, I forced myself to walk slowly into the kitchen, even as I wanted to rush in and throw myself at Jasmine. I didn't want them to know anything was wrong.

"Hey, Ericka." Sybil glanced up from the dishes she was washing with a smile. "What are you doing back down here? I thought you were given the night off of cleaning duty?"

I smiled back, but it was forced. "I was."

"Then what are you doing back here?" Jasmine turned from where she was instructing the others on tomorrow's menu and frowned, her hands on the swell of her hips. "I swear, you are a glutton for punishment. You just can't stop working, can you?"

I shrugged as I tucked a hair behind my ear. "What can I say? Idle hands and all that." Shifting on my feet as they stared at me, I moved further into the kitchen. "Actually, I'm not here to work."

Sybil frowned, lifted her hands out of the water, and dried them off on a towel. She and Jasmine walked toward me followed by Daphne and Margie. Sybil placed a hand on my arm, her brows drawn together with concern.

"Hey, what's wrong?"

Chewing on my lower lip, I offered her a weak smile. "I have to go home for a while, and I wanted to say goodbye."

"Home?" Jasmine took up the space on my other side, her eyes skimming my face for any signs of an answer. "Why? What happened?"

"Nothing." I shook my head and stepped out of their reach. "I just got word from my mother." I didn't like lying to them, but it was for their own good. I didn't want to put them in more danger by asking for their help. I pushed the words out in a rush. "My father is sick, and they fear he won't last the week. I want to be there for him before he..."

"No, no. Of course, we understand." Jasmine drew me into a tight embrace. "We wish you safe travels and health to your father and mother." Tears burned my eyes as she held me.

"Thank you." I nodded weakly. "Thank you so much for everything Jasmine. I know we didn't start out on the best of terms, but I think of you as one of my best friends."

"Ah, now look what you've done," Jasmine simpered, releasing me to wipe at her eyes. "Go on with you before you cause us all to start blubbering.

I nodded and turned to Sybil. "I'm sorry I got you into so much trouble. I really--"

"Nonsense." Sybil cut me off with a hug. "It's all in the past. Go take care of your family, and we'll see you when you come back. You are coming back right?"

I paused and then breathed out, "Yes, I'll see you again. I promise."

It wasn't a lie, not really. I did hope to see them again one day but not as one of them. Perhaps, I'd travel some. See Elphame like I always dreamed of. Then, after some time has passed and the king has found someone else to be obsessed over, I could come back. I hoped.

After I said my goodbyes, I walked toward the stables. There had to be a carriage on its way out to Boggsville or at least anywhere but here. I could find my way back home after I got off the palace grounds. It would be harder to find me if I was gone. A familiar silvery coat and translucent head of hair stood near a carriage being packed.

"Cailean!" I called out, hustling over to the half kelpie's side. "Please tell me that you are leaving soon."

Cailean's irisless eyes found me and a broad smile showed his sharp teeth. "Ericka Burner. It is good to see you." His eyes found my bag, and his lips turned down. "Leaving so soon?"

"Yes, things didn't exactly work out." I gripped my bag to my chest. That was an understatement. "Can you give me a ride?"

Understanding crossed Cailean's features, and he inclined his head. "Yes, but we're headed to Springdale on the border of the Summer Court. I'm afraid we won't be stopping in Boggsville any time soon, but it is on our course to pass by, if you don't mind riding along."

"I don't," I said quickly and then paused to smile. "I mean, I'm alright with a road trip. I've always wanted to see more of the Spring Court. Might as well do it while I'm young."

"My sentiments exactly." Cailean grinned, and his hand went to the carriage door, the other held out to me. "After you, m'lady."

Taking his offered hand, I climbed into the carriage as he opened the door. It was much smaller than the one I'd come in with the king. Not that I'd gotten a chance to ride in it. Though, I was sure riding inside would be a good bit better than riding up front. Even if the seats didn't have much cushion.

"We'll be leaving in just a moment. Make yourself comfortable."

I nodded at Cailean in thanks and shifted into my seat.

"Are you coming along too?" a young human woman with a snaggle toothed smile asked, her straw-colored hair braided in a crown around her head. "It'll be nice to have the company. I'm Bea." She held her freckled hand out to me.

I shook her outstretched hand and nodded. "Ericka."

Cailean banged on the top of the carriage to signal our departure, and a moment later, we were off. The carriage jolted and bumped along the pathway, and my stomach rolled. Maybe it wasn't much better than the outside.

"So..." Bea's eyes dipped to my bags and then to my face. "What are you running from?" She pronounced her r's with a growl, and there was a lilt to her voice that I couldn't place.

I hugged my bag to my lap and tucked my hair behind my ear, avoiding her gaze. "What makes you think I'm running?"

Bea laughed, a full-throated sound that included snorting. "I might be slow but I'm not daft. I know the look of a girl on the run. Was it a man or something else?"

I shifted in my seat, wincing as we hit a rather rough bumps in the road. "I don't want to talk about it."

"Ah," Bea drew out with a wink. "A man then. Come now, who was he?"

Seeing that I wasn't going to get out of talking to my unlikely companion for the duration of my trip, I tried to give her as little information as possible. "A fae."

"That's it then? All I get?" she chastised, and then mockingly said, "A fae. Bah, come on. There's got to be more to it than that. Did he bed you then leave you? Let me guess. He promised you riches beyond your imagination except what he really meant was riches of the heart and not of the pocket variety." She rubbed her fingers together with a grin.

"No." I said flatly. When she continued to grin at me, I sighed and gave up. "Honestly, he made my life at the palace a living hell except the couple of times that he was actually..." I dragged off not wanting to complete the sentence. "Any way, he went too far this time and I'm not going to take it anymore. So, I'm going home."

Bea leaned back in her chair and pursed her lips, watching me curiously. "What makes you think he won't come after you?"

I shrugged. "I don't but I have to try. I'm not special enough for him to make the effort. Besides, he has a kingdom to run." Bea's eyes widened and I realized what I'd said. Covering my mouth as I shook my head, I tried to fix it. "That's not what I meant. It's not the king. I mean, damn it all to hell and back. Just forget what I just said okay. Please?" I winced, begging with all my heart.

Unfortunately, Bea was not one so easily dissuaded. "It's you!" She pointed a finger at me with glee. "You're that kitchen girl who has the king's crown jewels all in a twist. Oh, my gods. I'm so excited to meet you!" She practically vibrated in her seat at the information.

"You've heard of me?" I cringed, not liking that someone I didn't even know until today knew who I was, if not by name but by association with the king.

"Of course, I do! Everyone in the palace was talking about it. I only work in laundry but even we hear tidbits. About how he picked you out of all the other cooks because you threw a pie in his face. About how he loved your pie so much that he brought you home with him." She wagged her brows suggestively making me groan. "I even know that your room is in the same hallway as his. He doesn't let any servants let alone humans live that close to him! You must really be special."

I leaned my elbow on the carriage window and slapped my chin into my hand. "Oh, yeah. So lucky. I'm rolling in it as you can see."

Bea's happiness dimmed a bit. "Come now, it can't be all that bad. Everyone from here to the Winter Court is dying to catch the eye of King Balefire. I bet he is quite the wicked lover, isn't he?" She winked like we had a secret.

I felt bad for the girl. I was about to burst her little sex filled dreams about the so-called king. "Actually, I wouldn't know. We've never even kissed let alone had sex. The only action we've ever gotten was him threatening me or trying to kill me. Which I guess could be considered foreplay if you look at it from a fae perspective." I laughed sadly.

Bea placed a hand to her face, tapping her chin with her fingers. "Hmmm, that doesn't sound the king I'd heard about. Maybe you caught him on a bad day?"

I let out a bitter chuckle. "A bad month perhaps." I took a deep breath and sighed. "Look, I know you want to think he's this damaged king who just wants to be loved but that's not the man, that's not the fae I've seen. Besides, he has Shirazan."

She made a disgusted face. "The dragon? Ew."

I laughed freely this time. "Not like that. She can turn humanoid. And they're...lovers, I guess?" My eyes went to the ceiling of the carriage and I shook my head. "I don't know. In any case, I don't want to be in the middle of it. Whatever it is. It's better for me to just leave."

"But that's not going to fix the problem just delay it." Bea argued leaning forward to place a hand on my knee. "If you are as important to him as everyone keeps saying, he won't just let you disappear. He's going to come after you."

I smiled darkly. "He'll have to find me first."

As if waiting for me to say that very thing, there was a loud crack and then Bea and I were thrown to the side. The carriage leaned precariously on its side as we picked ourselves up off the floor of the carriage. Groaning, I rubbed my head and carefully peeked out the window.

"Cailean? Is everything alright?"

Cailean's translucent face appeared in the window, irritation pinched his face. "We broke a wheel. I'm afraid it's going to take a little while to fix."

"Oh, no." I frowned placing a hand up to my face. "Should we go for help?" I looked to Bea for her thoughts.

Bea glanced out the window and then slowly opened the door climbing out. The carriage swayed as her weight left the vehicle. Following suit, I inched my way to the door and stepped out onto the shimmering crystal paved road. A large blue crystal jutted out of the ground where the wheel was broken at the rim.

"If I'm right there's a village just on the other side of those trees." Bea pointed toward the east where a bundle of glistening green and purple trees stood. "It's not a big village more like a hole in the wall but there should be someone there to at least help fix the wheel."

Turning my attention to Cailean, I shrugged. "Better than nothing, I suppose."

Cailean looked around and scratched the side of his head before shrugging as well. "Alright well, let's see what we can find."

"What about the carriage?" I pointed to the luggage attached to it. "Someone might steal it."

Waving me off, Cailean tapped the side of the carriage and a barrier glimmered around the whole of it. "Don't worry, it's spelled. Anyone who tries to steal from it will be in for a nasty shock."

Satisfied, I walked toward the direction of the village. "Alright then, let's do this."

Chapter 20

Balefire

IT WAS DINNER BY the time I was able to get away to search for Ericka. I tried to push it off onto Finch or even Bartholomew, but the Banshees were from the Winter Court and their queen was as frigid as their court. Nothing short of a personal letter from the king as well as a gift of apology for the inconvenience, which to her would be all the killing of a banshee coven would be. That too had to be handpicked.

What did you give the Queen of an ice desert? An ice pick? Eventually, I settled on a blue and white rose from the royal gardens. My mother would have been pissed if she knew but I was in a hurry and wasn't about to spend days finding the right gift.

Finally done with my task, I could go about getting back on Ericka's good side. If that were all possible. I'd really made a mess of things this time.

Sitting at the dining table alone, I tapped my fork against the top of the table, impatiently hoping to see Ericka. I hoped by now the human had enough time to calm down from what happened with us before.

How long did a human need to get over almost being fed to a dragon? A few hours? Days? I hoped it wouldn't take that long. Shirazan would make her move against Ericka soon, and I wanted to be sure she was with me before it happened.

I hadn't heard from Shirazan since I left her in my room. I hadn't been back to my room either. I'd changed in Finch's room and wore one of his shirts which was a smidge too small and pulled across my chest muscles. Not that anyone has commented on it. I did notice that I had a lot more eyes on me since I put on Finch's skintight pants. The serving women in their crimson dresses were eyeing me from the side of the room. I didn't need to have enhanced sense of smell to tell that they were wafting pheromones all over the place.

With an annoyed grunt, I turned my gaze back to the table. A roasted duck sitting in pixie tears and pineapple juice sat in the middle of the table. Honey and cinnamon glazed carrots sat in a bowl off to the side. The servants had tried to serve me, but I had waved them off, choosing to only drink the huckleberry fairy wine instead. My stomach was a mess. There was no way I could eat any of the food before I talk to Ericka, even if she had a hand in the food on the table. At least the wine was taking some of my edge off. Maybe I would hold my temper long enough to explain about Shirazan. Apologize for...well so many things.

I let out a long sigh.

"Something I can do for you, your majesty?" The only male server, a faun, appeared at my side. I glanced up from the inside of my glass, wondering how I hadn't noticed him approach me. My mind must really be off today.

I shook my head. "No. I'm fine."

"Is the food not to your liking?" The curly brown headed faun nodded toward the meal before me. His pointed ears twitched, a telling sign that he was nervous about my answer.

Turning my eyes to the food and then back to the faun, I shook my head. "Everything looks great. I guess I'm just not that hungry."

The faun nodded and stepped back. He then motioned to the two serving women who came to clear the table. The faun turned to leave, but I grabbed his arm as I thought of something.

"Your name is Luke, correct?"

I could tell I'd caught the faun off guard as his brows lifted and his eyes widened.

"Uh, yes, Your Majesty." Confusion filled his voice.

Leaning back in my seat, I placed an elbow on the armrest of my chair, surveying him closely.

"You worked with the other one. The human woman."

Luke licked his lips, and his eyes flitted to the side to the other servant women who tried to hide a shake of their heads. The moment he decided he wasn't going to tell me anything, his back straightened, and his jaw tightened. When he spoke, his voice no longer wavered and had a sharpness to it that it didn't have before.

"I do not know who you're talking about, your majesty. We have so many servants come in and out of your employment, human and fae alike. It is hard to remember them all."

There was a lie in there somewhere, one that the faun had carefully tried to conceal. I decided not calling him out on it and tried another tactic.

"The human I am looking for goes by the name of Ericka Burner." His ears twitched at Ericka's name, but he didn't speak yet. I hadn't asked a question, so he didn't think he had to. The two others shot Luke a worried look before taking their plates and hurrying toward the kitchen door, leaving him to my wrath. "Now before you try to walk around my question, I know you know who she is. I remember you talking to her the night Lady Nico had dinner here. Now, I haven't run into Ericka since earlier today, but I have a feeling you know where she is."

Luke opened his mouth to answer, but I cut him off with a warning look.

"Don't try and evade the question. Where is Ericka Burner?"

Clipping his mouth shut, Luke's brows furrowed and his cheek twitches. After a moment, he decided what he was going to tell me. "I haven't seen her today."

"But someone must have," I prodded further, shifting so that my hands laced in front of me on the table. I glanced down at the table and sighed, praying for patience. "Who saw her last? And where is she now?"

Squirming in place, the faun looked anywhere but at me.

"Tell me, faun." I banged my hand on the table, the sound causing the faun to jump in place. Counting down from ten, I let a long breath out and rubbed my forehead. "I'm not going to punish you. I just want to know where she is." I struggled with the next word. "Please."

"I don't know where she is." Luke began wringing his hands in front of him. When I sighed in frustration and about to bang my hand on the table again, he rushed out, "But I do know she came to the kitchens earlier with a bag in her hands. She was leaving." Sadness filled his voice.

I wasn't sad though, I was furious. I jerked to my feet, which sent my chair flying back to smash into the wall.

"What do you mean she was leaving? Where did she go?"

Luke backed up quickly, shaking his head from side to side. "I... I don't know. You'd have to talk to the cook, Jasmine. She would know."

My gaze darted to the revolving door, and my eyes narrowed. "I'll do just that."

The faun sagged in relief as I stalked by him and toward the kitchen. I pushed the door open hard enough that it banged against the wall. The sound reverberated through the room, and the chattering in the room instantly went quiet. My gaze scanned the room quickly and zeroed in on the cerulean-haired fae.

Jasmine had her hands full of pots, and it looked like she was in the middle of moving them to the cabinet but stopped when I appeared. I didn't need to ask the question of where Ericka was because the look on her face said everything I needed to know.

She was gone. Ericka had left, and she hadn't even said goodbye.

Rage, frustration, and if I was honest with myself, despair whirled inside of me. How could she have left like that? Where had she gone?

Who was I kidding? Why wouldn't she leave after what I did to her? I was surprised she hadn't left before.

Shaking my head at my own stupidity, I rubbed my hand over my face and groaned out, "Please tell me you know where she went."

Jasmine placed the pots down on the counter and stepped toward me. Her eyes narrowed on me, she crossed her arms over her apron-clad body. "Why should I tell you?"

A few of the servants gasped at Jasmine's answer. They were right to be afraid for her. Speaking to me that way was an automatic trip to the dungeon. However, this time, Jasmine's ire was justified. Trying my best to keep my voice steady and not to lose my temper, I approached her, my hands out in an offer of peace.

"Please, I need to find her. Just tell me where she went."

Jasmine struggled for a moment, and confusion crossed her face at my words. It wasn't surprising that she didn't trust my unusual behavior. I was more of a punish first and ask questions later kind of person. This time, though, I had something to lose, and I couldn't be rash or threaten my way out of this one.

"You care for her." A red headed freckled fae stepped out from behind the counter, her brows drawn down and her lips twisted in a frown. I couldn't remember her name, something like Mary or Maggie. There were too many of them to remember. Whatever-her-name was bound and determined to get me to answer the next question she asked. "Do you love her?"

I opened my mouth, and no words came out. Did I? I didn't know. I knew I couldn't bear the thought of her being gone but as far as love was concerned... I didn't know. I just didn't know.

"You don't have to answer that." Jasmine held her hand up and closed the distance between us. "Ericka came here earlier with a bag in her hand. She said she had a family emergency and might not be back for a while. But looking at you," her eyes trailed over my face as if searching for something, "I have a feeling it was something else."

"So, she went home?" I couldn't hold back the hope in my voice. I could go to Boggsville. I could find her and explain. Hopefully, I could even convince her to come back.

"She said her father was sick. I would assume that means she went back to Boggsville." Jasmine glanced toward the clock on the wall and hummed. "It's only been about half an hour since she left. You might still be able to catch her on the main road."

I grabbed her by the shoulders, which caused her to stiffen. "You have my gratitude." My gaze went around the room. "All of you."

Releasing Jasmine, I marched out of the kitchen and toward my bedroom. If I was going to go after Ericka, I needed to change. I wasn't getting on a horse with pants that might split at any moment. It wasn't until I arrived at my bedroom door that I remembered Shirazan might still be in there waiting for me. Gods above, help me. I did not have the time or patience to deal with her right now.

After a moment spent preparing myself for an argument, I opened the bedroom door and walked into the room. The light was off which was a good sign. I flicked it on and skimmed my room. She wasn't here. Good.

Not wasting anymore time, I rushed to my wardrobe and threw on my riding pants and a tunic. Then I shoved my feet into my riding boots, grabbed my jacket, and pulled it on as I made for the door. I'd have to take a horse. It was the quickest way to get to her in time. I could only assume she hadn't opted to walk to Boggsville and had caught a ride with one of the various carriages that came and went from the palace daily. I should be able to catch up with them fairly easy.

I moved for the door but then stopped at the sight of the hand mirror sitting on the side table. Of course, how could I have forgotten about it? I had been so frazzled by the banshees and what happened with Ericka earlier that I had forgotten all about using the magic mirror to find her.

Picking the mirror up, I turned it over my hand. The surface had several long cracks in it. My heart sank and then anger flare in my belly.

Shirazan.

It had to be her who had done this. That conniving bitch. The mirror wouldn't work now with a crack through it. I'd have to take it to the court sorcerer to have it fixed later. With an annoyed growl, I tossed the mirror onto the nearby chair and turned on my heels. I'd have to find Ericka the old fashion way.

On my way to the stables, I stopped by Finch's room to return his clothing and tell him my plan.

"So, you're going after her?" Finch asked with a smug grin. "It took you long enough to figure out how you feel about her. I was beginning to think you were dropped on your head as a child."

"That's beside the point." I shook my head and backed towards Finch's door. "I have to find her, explain what happened, and beg her to come back."

"Beg? You?" Finch chuckled and stood. "I have to see that. I'm coming too."

I narrowed my eyes at him and growled out, "Fine, but if you slow me down, I will leave you behind."

Finch snorted. "Out of the two of us, who is the better rider?"

I didn't answer his redundant question as we made quick time getting to the stables. When we arrived, it was obvious something was off. There weren't many servants around, and the ones that were there had huddled into a little group off to the side. A wagon laid overturned, and scorch marks covered the side of it. The usual horses that were known to be around waiting to be attached to wagons and carriages were suspiciously missing.

Finch hurried over to the group of servants, and in hushed voices, they rapidly answered his questions. The servants tossed fearful looks in my direction, and when Finch was done, they dispersed. Finch walked back over to me with a frown marring his mouth.

"What happened?" I prodded, knowing I wasn't going to like the answer.

"Your pet dragon happened. I told you it was a bad idea to give her so much freedom."

"Shirazan?" My mouth fell open as I surveyed the damage once more. Now that I knew what to look for, it definitely seemed like something large had rampaged through here. The scorch marks should have tipped me off right away. "Why would she do this?"

"I don't know." Finch ran a hand through his pale hair and scowled. "Someone said she came in here hell bent on running off any horses she could. She didn't even bother with the servants. It was like she was making sure no one could leave here today."

Something tickled at the back of my mind. "Where did she go?"

Finch pointed toward the east. "That way."

"But there's nothing but trees and forest in that direction." I stroked my chin and tried to puzzle out the predicament before me. "The closest village isn't for at least a day's ride. Why would she go that way?"

"Actually," Finch interrupted my thoughts, "there's a small village on the other side of those trees. Not many go there because it's just a few houses and a farm, but it's there. Maybe she knows something we don't?"

My eyes widened. "Ericka!"

"What?"

I grabbed Finch by the arms and shook him. "She must have figured out before we did that Ericka had gone that way."

"Why would she care about her? Last I heard, Shirazan was eating out of the palm of your hand." His eyes dipped down to my pants and he smirked. "So to speak."

I shook my head and cursed. "Not since today when I told her I was done with her."

"You did what?" Finch gaped and then chuckled bitterly. "After all these years, I've been telling you to get rid of her, and you finally do it today of all days. Why?"

My lips twisted to the side, and I kicked at the ground as I muttered, "Ericka walked in on us."

"Please tell me you are joking." Finch looked ready to wrap his hands around my throat, and I didn't blame him. It wasn't something I had wanted Ericka to see. Especially, when I didn't really want to be there with Shirazan anyway.

I sighed and stared off toward the east. "I wish I was. However, in my defense I did push her off before anything could escalate."

"Fine. Fine. You messed up. We'll fix it, but first, we have to save the damsel." Finch placed his hands on his hips and searched around the stables. "Where are we going to get a horse?"

The tattoos on my chest pulsated with powers as I stared hard in the direction Shirazan and Ericka went. I had to get to her, and I had to get to her now. The tattoos on my skin blazed brightly, burning away my shirt as my skin itched. I flexed my arms as the power pushed at my back and head. Pain ripped through as my flesh tore and long wings sprouted from my back. Horns pushed through my skull and curled toward the sky.

"Bale," Finch cautiously stepped forward, his eyes on my wings and horns, "are you sure this is a good idea? You know what happened last time. You don't have complete control over yourself in this form."

I tested my wings, my back muscles contracting and releasing. A low gurgling growl slipped from between my clenched teeth.

"I have no choice."

Without waiting for Finch to speak again, I took to the skies, my mind on one thing: Ericka.

Chapter 21

Ericka

I STARED OFF INTO the horizon and sighed for what seemed like the hundredth time. The sun had sunk further in the distance and what was supposed to be an easy fix ended up being more complicated than we thought.

Freddie, the man who could have helped up fix our wheel and be on our way, had been called away and wouldn't be back until evening. Well, the evening came and went, and still no sign of the elusive Freddie. With each minute that passed, my nerves ratched up even more.

"Oh, baby, look at that sunset," Bea mused. "Ain't that the prettiest thing you've ever seen?"

I jumped in my seat, spinning around to stare up at Bea. "Huh? What?"

"A bit jumpy, huh?" Bea, my new unlikely companion, chuckled and plopped down on a seat next to me at the long table the little village used for their evening dinners.

The concept of community was big with the villagers, all of them brownies, and it made my heart ache for my own little community I'd left behind. I glanced away from the woman and back toward the setting sun.

"Uh, yeah. It's pretty," I muttered, my heart really not into it. The longer we stayed here, the more likely that Balefire would catch up with me, and the last thing I wanted right now was a confrontation with him.

Understanding blossomed on Bea's face and she nodded with a sly grin. "But it's not the sight you'd rather be seeing, is it?"

"No. Sorry." I sighed and pressed the heel of my hand against my eyes to soothe the ache there. "It's great. Just really wanted to be further away from the palace by now."

"No, no," Bea insisted with a wave of her hands. "I get it. Running from your problems and all that. I can hardly expect you are enjoying our little side trip. Still..." Her gaze drifted over the little village.

Really it was less of a village and more of a cluster of houses. I counted six houses all bundled together, with the surrounding trees squeezing in between. A barn and a fenced-in area housing horses, sheep, and chicken sat on the opposite side of the clearing. They had made the center of their little village a fire pit with an old-style cooking pot hanging from metal rods over the now-lit fire.

The village had a certain homey feel to it, a simpler feel that made me wish I could have come there for another reason, one that didn't require me to be checking the time so often. As it were, every time someone came by or I heard hooves on the road, my heart jumped into my throat, and my pulse raced. It was only a matter of time before Balefire came after me... if he came after me. I still wasn't so sure, but Bea seemed to think that I was someone worth coming after. She meant it as a compliment, but it was not one that I really cared for at the moment.

"How much longer do you think it'll be?" I asked as I glanced toward the carriage.

Cailean had gotten into the clearing with some help from the local brownies. He was having a merry old time chatting up the locals. They were in awe of a half-kelpie which made Cailean feel much like royalty when he was used to being ignored or even sneered at.

I was happy for him, I really was, but all this time here was making me lose that much more time to get away. If this Freddie fellow didn't show up by nightfall, I'd have to find another way to go on. I couldn't go back to the palace, but there was supposed to be another village further ahead, one with more carriages that could take me to my next destination or, at least, get me further from the palace.

"Who knows?" Bea leaned back in her chair, her legs thrown out in front of her, ankles crossed over each other as she laced her hands on top of her yellow mop of hair. "Could be tomorrow before it gets fixed."

My jaw tightened at her words. Tomorrow. I couldn't wait until tomorrow. I needed to be gone now.

I sat by the fire with Bea for a few moments longer, trying to work out how to get to my next destination when the woods around us grew quiet. Unnaturally quiet. Then I heard it. The flapping of wings. Large wings by the way the wind blew hazardously through the village.

Everyone stopped what they were doing and stared up at the sky. The light that had been left from the setting sun was suddenly blotted out, leaving only the torches and fire pit to keep us out of complete darkness. That shadow that darkened the sky had the distinctive shape of something familiar.

"Dragon!" a nearby villager shouted as he pointed up at the sky and then darted into his home.

I jumped to my feet as everything went into chaos. The villagers scrambled out of the way, running into their homes and the woods around us. Bea stared in horror up at the immense form of the dragon coming toward us fast.

With wings made of night and a long neck and tail whipping back and forth as it searched the ground, the dragon's raze claw clenched and unclenched as if preparing to grab something or someone nearby. I had a feeling I knew what. The glowing green eyes of the dragon zeroed in on the village as it descended even faster. Its large body made a shadow that covered the ground in night, its scales the same bottomless black as its wings shimmered with the dying light.

Move!" I shouted at her which woke her up enough to get her to panic. Clamping my mouth shut, I gave Bea a shove to get her feet moving.

There was only one dragon that I knew, Shirazan, and she didn't like me too much. Actually, she didn't like me at all. Besides, the fact that she thought I was taking the king away from her had driven her to try to kill me once already. That made the bad feeling in my stomach justified. There was no way this was a coincidence.

Bea and I darted behind the broken-down carriage, and I peeked out through one of the unbroken wheel's spokes. Cailean jumped down next to us moments later, his second set of eyelids opening and closing rapidly as he tried to regain his breath.

"What is the king's dragon doing here?" Cailean asked, his lips pressed into a thin line.

Bea shot a look in my direction. "I don't know. Maybe she decided she had a taste for brownies?"

"Bea!" I smacked the woman next to me on the arm and scowled. "That's a horrible thing to say."

"Better than the alternative," Bea muttered, her gaze sliding toward Cailean.

"What's she talking about?" Cailean inquired, his head canted to the side as he stared at the two of us suspiciously.

"Nothing," I reassured him with another shake of my head. "She's got a wild imagination."

"Ericka," Shirazan's sultry voice called out in a singsong manner. "Come out, pet. I just want to talk."

I snorted. Fat chance.

Bea shot me a look. "See? I told you."

"Told her what?" Cailean glanced between the two of us as confusion marred his face. "Ericka, what does the king's dragon want with you?"

"Likely to eat me." I gritted my teeth and glared through the wheel at the dark-haired fae sauntered around the campfire. Shirazan had shed her dragon form and stalked around the clearing in one of those body fitting dresses she seemed to be so fond of. Her eyes glittered in the failing light, her lips tipped up to reveal her sharpened canines.

"Don't make this harder than it needs to be, dear," Shirazan crooned. "I know you are here. Either you come out or..." Her eyes turned red, and she opened her mouth wide. Flames burst forth and caught a bale of silvery hay on fire.

The horses nearby neighed in alarm and rushed to the other side of the fenced in area but couldn't go any further. The chickens crowed their displeasure as the sheep baa'd incessantly. Still, I stayed where I was.

"If you won't come out on your own, I guess I will just have to flush you out." Shirazan tapped her chin with her long black nails before turning her attention toward one of the nearby houses. Her eyes glowed red, and I knew what she intended to do.

"No! Stop!" I jumped to my feet and rushed around the carriage before Bea or Cailean had the chance to stop me. "You don't need to hurt any of these people. I'm here. Let's talk."

Shirazan grinned broadly, those sharp canines making her smile wicked. "There you are, human. Brave of you to come forward. Smart too. We wouldn't want innocent bystanders to get in the way of our... discussion."

Sure, we wouldn't. If Shirazan only wanted to talk to me, I was a hippogriff.

"What do you want, Shirazan? Shouldn't you be with the king, you know...'talking.'" I used air quotes around the word and I shifted my feet in preparation for whatever she threw at me. Or in this case, blew at me. Of all the ways I expected I might die, burning alive wasn't one of them. Food poisoning from one of my own dishes, yeah, but dragon fire, yeah not even my parents would have guessed that one.

Shirazan's eyes narrowed, the smile on her lips dying. "No, actually. The king and I won't be talking anymore. No thanks to you." She stalked toward me watching me like the reptile that she was.

I side stepped until the fire pit was between us. Not that I thought it would stop her. "That sounds like your problem not mine. I don't want the king. So have at it."

A dark chuckle slid past her lips as she smirked. "It doesn't matter what you want you wretched human. The king wants you and that's all that matters. And as long as he does he will no longer turn to me to fulfill his needs."

My nose scrunched up in disgust. "Well, I'm leaving, so you don't have to worry about it anymore. I'm sure he'll forget all about me and be happy to let you..." I swallowed thickly, not able to stomach the words coming from my mouth. "... you know."

"It doesn't matter how far you go, the king will find you." Shirazan lifted a clawed hand up and examined her fingernails with a bored expression. "And believe me, you may say you don't want him, but he can be rather persuasive when he wants to be." She paused and slid her hands down her form until they landed on her hips. "How do you think he got me?"

"He just whistled?" The words popped out of my mouth before I could stop them, and I had about a millisecond to dodge before the dragon bitch roasted me alive.

"Stop moving, you insufferable leech," Shirazan screamed at me, stalking around the fire pit to come after me.

I didn't give her the chance to catch me as I rushed around the barn and into the woods.

Shirazan's voice carried to me as she shouted, "I will burn this whole forest down and you with it to get what I want! Be a good little human, and die with some dignity."

I snorted. Like I had any dignity left to give.

I scrambled behind a tree, my heart thudding against my chest as I caught my breath. She wouldn't really do it, would she? Kill all these trees just to get to me? It didn't take long before I had my answer. Flames roared into the sky, and the scent of wood and glass burning hit my nose, making me sneeze. I pulled the front of my dress up over my nose and tried not to breathe in the fumes.

Peeking around the tree I hid behind, a wall of fire sat before me. It spread like wildfire, because it basically was, and her threat of burning the whole place down just to get to me became all too real. I turned from the fire and ran further into the trees, hoping to outrun the flames. Of course, my foot caught on a branch, and I went sprawling into a clearing.

Seconds later, a dark shadow fell over me, and a looming presence came rapidly for me. There was no time to run, so I tried to make myself as small as possible and squeezed my eyes shut against the pain that was to come.

"Ericka," a familiar growl called out my name, and I chanced a peek up at the shadow. It wasn't a dragon, but it didn't seem like anything I'd ever seen before. Except the face. The face I knew all too well.

Balefire.

"What are you doing here?" I hurried to my feet and rushed towards him. "How did you find me? What the hell happened to you?"

My mouth fell open as the nearby fires illuminated Balefire's new form. Large wings spread out a good five feet or more on either side of his back. Golden horns protruded from his head, curling up about a foot in the air. He was missing his shirt and the tattoos on his chest and arm glowed an ethereal yellow against his skin. Those gorgeous blue eyes of his seemed to be alive with energy as they assessed me.

When he didn't speak, I cautiously walked toward him. My hand reached up and touched the glowing tattoos on his chest. I didn't know why I was being so forward. I never would have touched him on my own accord before, but there was something about him now, sometimes different. Perhaps, it was the way his nostrils flared at my nearness or how his chest muscles shuddered under my palm, but I had to make him know it was okay. As my hands moved over his chest and cupped his face, I made shushing sounds like one would to a baby.

"It's alright," I cooed. "You're okay. I'm okay."

Balefire's eyes locked on me, then he huffed a grunt and grabbed me around the waist. My spine stiffened, and I instinctively wanted to tell him to get his hands off of me but held back. He wasn't himself right now, that much was clear. The Balefire I knew would have been talking my ear off by now. The man loved the sound of his own voice. However, this version of him watched me like a predatory watched its prey.

Unfortunately, I wasn't sure what kind of prey he was looking for. The food kind or... the other kind. I didn't particularly want to be either. I opened my mouth to tell him so, but his head jerked to the side back toward the village. All of a sudden, his wings beat behind him, and his grasp on me tightened.

"What are you--" I didn't get the full question out before my feet were lifted from the ground, and we were soaring through the sky. A scream caught in my throat, but I clamped down on it. I wrapped my arms around his neck and clung to him closer than I ever would have dared before.

The ground grew further away, and I wondered briefly how far up he was going to take us when Shirazan's dragon form came bounding out of the fire-lit trees. The black scales on her body hid most of her in the shadows, as the sun had set during our chase. Her long spiked tail whipped from one side to the other, knocking glass trees over, and their leaves and branches shattered on impact. She sniffed the ground where I'd once laid before her eyes shot up to the sky.

A long, loud roar erupted from her throat as her wings pounded against the air, lifting her up and off the ground. Balefire didn't seem bothered by her approach nor did he release me. Shirazan, however, saw me clutching onto the king, and her eyes glowed red. I cowered against him, sure of what was coming, but Balefire simply turned his back on her. Warmth came from behind us, and I lifted myself up to see over his shoulders.

His wings, they blocked the attack from Shirazan. The dragon's flames being absorbed into the long golden feathers on his back. Busy gasping in surprise, I didn't even notice what happened next until Balefire was already barrel rolling us toward the ground. I squeezed my eyes shut and let out a long horrified scream as we descended. When we jerked to a stop, a choking gasp poured out of me.

Balefire suddenly released me on to my feet. He must have landed, because I collapsed on the ground instead of falling to my doom. I stared up at him in partly in awe and partly in terror, and Balefire locked his glowing gaze with mine.

"Stay." The word came out in a snarl right before he lifted up into the sky once more.

I could do nothing but watch from the ground as he went to face Shirazan.

The dragon tried to descend as well, but Balefire rushed at her, pushing her up and away from me. At least he was in his right mind enough to know who the bad guy was. I could count my blessings for that.

"Ericka!"

My eyes jerked away from the scene of the fight above me to the charcoaled trees. Cailean, Bea, and Finch rushed toward me. While Bea and Cailean pulled up a few feet away, Finch came to kneel at my side.

"Are you alright?" His usual jovial smile was turned down with worry.

"I'm fine." I waved him off and tucked my hair behind me ears as I worked my way up to my knees and then my feet. "How did you and Balefire even find me?"

A loud roar above made the ground quake, and we all looked to the sky. Balefire had his arms around Shirazan's massive neck, and she wasn't too happy about it. I wanted to help him, but there was nothing I could do from the ground. I flinched as Shirazan swiped her tail at him, hitting him repeatedly in the back until he released her. I winced.

"His Majesty found out where you were going from Jasmine." Finch began pulling my gaze from the fight for a moment. "When we went to get horses to go after you, they were all chased away by Shirazan." Finch paused and his lips pressed into a thin line. "Balefire used his family's magic to change forms to get to you faster."

"Why would he do that?" I frowned hard, my eyes narrowing as I squinted to see the fight. "I'm not really worth all this hassle, am I?"

Bea scoffed and shook her head. "Please tell her the king is head over heels for her. She won't believe me."

I glared at her before turning back to Finch. "It's ridiculous. There's no way he..." Finch simply gave me a pointed look, and my brows furrowed in confusion. "But why? I'm nothing special."

Finch and Cailean shared a look before they both broke out into a chuckle.

"The heart wants what it wants." Finch placed a hand on my shoulder. "His Majesty isn't very good at showing his emotions, and the majority of time, they even elude him. Believe me, he wouldn't be here if he didn't think you were worth it."

My gaze trailed back up to the sky and the raging battle I couldn't help with. I worried my bottom lip between my teeth as I tried to figure out what the fae before me could ever see in me. And why in the hell hadn't he told me?

Chapter 22

Balefire

MY BACK ACHED FROM the lashes it had taken from Shirazan. My power waned, and I knew I couldn't maintain this form for much longer. Still, I pushed down my fatigue and tightened my hold on Shirazan's neck. I couldn't stop now. She had to die, not just for attacking Ericka, but for what she threatened to my kingdom and my people.

Shirazan roared and tried to breathe fire on me again. but my own powers blocked it. In this case, she couldn't fight fire with fire. Of the two of us, my fire was far more powerful than hers and all the more lethal.

As my exhaustion grew, I flew out of the reach of her tail and her long neck. I had to end this before it went any further, and that's when my gaze slipped down to where Ericka and the others waited.

It was all the distraction Shirazan needed. Her claw lashed out and caught me across the chest. I cried out and grabbed my chest as it burned in pain. My mind back in the moment, I managed to dodge her next attack, even as blood seeped down my chest and arms.

Her roar of frustration was the only thing that kept me going. I should have put her down a long time ago. I should never have taken her in as some kind of pet that I hoped to tame. She was a dragon. A beast.

Just like I was.

My wings allowed me to hover in the air, flapping steadily behind me as I lifted my hands and summoned up the rest of my magic to unleash upon her. The power built up in my chest, and it felt as though it was burning through my veins, my flesh, everything. As the flames exploded out of my hands, I screamed. My scream was quickly followed by that of Shirazan, as the dragon couldn't resist against my magical flames. Nothing could.

Her wings gave out on her and she rushed toward the ground, breaking trees and bones as she fell. With a sickening crunch, she plowed hard into the earth. She tried to rise feebly once, but then collapsed on the ground in a heap of burning scales and flesh.

A sigh and a grunt escaped my throat before my wings gave out, and then I too was falling. The wind fluttered against my hair as I fell down, down, and then there was nothing but darkness.

When I awoke, my body burned with my intense exertion. It was as if every part of me had been stretched beyond capacity and then shoved back into a very small shell. I groaned and shifted. The ground was so soft... too soft to be the dirt and rock I'd landed on. I struggled to open my eyes and a cool hand touched my forehead, a soothing voice shushing me.

"It's alright. You're safe. Just sleep."

I didn't have the energy to fight the command, so I fell back into unconsciousness. The blackness of unconsciousness shifted into the dreams of sleep for a while. I was back in the garden with Ericka, but this time, there was no yelling or threats of death. We were laying before the encased rose, and she wrapped up in my arms. She giggled at something I said and snuggled in closer. I didn't remember the rest, but I was at peace.

The light hurt my eyes when they fluttered open at last. I squinted against the brightness and lifted a hand up to cover my eyes. My body still hurt but not as much as before. White bandages were wrapped around the arm I lifted, and with a cursory feel, I could tell that they were all over the rest of my body.

Pushing to a seated position as my eyes adjusted, I searched around the small barren room. Besides the tiny bed that I had been shoved onto that left my feet hanging over the edges, there was only a single stand next to the bed. On that stand sat a glass of water. I quickly grabbed it even though the sudden motion caused my back to scream in protest.

After I gulped down its contents, I sighed and sat back on the bed. I contemplated moving, but the world started to spin. Taking slow shallow breaths, I waited until I didn't feel like my stomach would reject the water I had just drank before slowly sitting back up.

I shifted, inching my legs over the side of the bed until I was able to stand. The door to the room opened, and Ericka's dark eyes landed on me. They widened a fraction before she rushed to my side. That's when I noticed the bowl of steaming hot soup in her hands, which she sat on the side table before giving my shoulder a little nudge.

"You shouldn't be up yet, Your Majesty," she chastised me as I allowed her to sit me back on the bed. "You're not well enough yet."

"I feel fine," I croaked out, but I still let her fuss over me some more.

As she did so, I watched her face closely, searching for any sign of pain. When I found none, I sagged in relief. She was alright. I'd gotten to her in time.

"What happened?" I asked at last.

Ericka paused in her task of tucking me back into bed and lifted her head to meet my gaze. "You don't remember?"

I shook my head and then winced at the action. "I can't always control my beast when I unleash it."

"Got it." She nodded and sighed, before she clasped her hands together and stepped back from the bed. "Well, you kicked Shirazan's butt and then, because you're a right bastard determined to send me to an early grave, you almost killed yourself falling from the sky."

My lips twitched at her blatant insult. "Is that right? You weren't worried for me, were you, Ericka?"

Ericka's eyes darted to mine and then to the side as she frowned. "No, of course not. You're the king. We can't have you breaking your royal neck for a commoner, let alone a human. What would I say to everyone had you died, hm?"

"You're not just some human, Ericka," I argued and then, when she made to move away, I grasped her wrist. "And I'm not just the king."

Ericka frowned at my grip but allowed herself to be drawn back to my side. "You *are* the king, though, and you shouldn't have put yourself in danger for me."

"Because you're not worth it?" I arched a brow at her.

"Exactly." She jerked her head up and down, then tried to pull away. "You yourself tried to kill me before, so why bother trying to save me now? Besides, now you've lost one of your valuable defenses. Who would fear you now?"

"I don't think I have a problem making others fear me." I smirked. "I never had any problems before Shirazan came to the palace. However, I feel like we've gotten off point."

"And what point might that be?" Ericka sighed her frustration and rubbed her free hand over her face. "Because I'm at a loss. Everyone keeps telling me that you have some kind of morbid attraction to me, but since I arrived at the palace, all you've done is drive me crazy. Then you almost got me killed by Shirazan, before almost getting killed by the same exact dragon you just defeated for me... again. What is your game? Because frankly? I'm too tired to play."

"There's no game." I stroked my thumb up and down the side of her wrist, enjoying the way her pulse jumped at my touch. "Not anymore."

"So, did I win?"

I laughed, startling her as it caused pain through my ribs. "I suppose you could put it that way." I smiled up at her cheekily. "Let's just say that I was playing for a whole other reward than your surrender."

"So, I've been told," she muttered as she stared down at where our hands were touching. "I'll just go get Finch for you, Your Majesty."

"Balefire."

"What?" She stopped, looking back at me curiously.

"Call me Balefire," I told her and reached for her hand again. "And I wanted to apologize."

Frowning down at me, she shifted closer. "Apologize for what?"

I shifted uncomfortably in the bed and winced again when stabs of pain were the result. Still, I pulled her closer to me, regardless of the pain, and reached up to touch the side of her face. She didn't flinch away which was a good sign. Steeling myself, I took a deep breath and spilled my truth.

"I wanted to apologize for everything. For mistreating you the way I did, not allowing you to do your job, which, let's be honest, hurt both of us," I chuckled and shook my head, "I don't think I can go back to eating just Jasmine's cooking."

She giggled lightly at that. "No, I suppose not."

"I also wanted to apologize for the way I reacted in the garden and for everything after that..." I trailed off and searched her eyes. "I can be reckless and jump to decisions without thinking them through."

Ericka snorted. "Don't forget stubborn and a right pain in the ass."

"No." I grinned at her. "We can't forget those."

Her lips twisted to the side, Ericka watched me for a moment before nodding. "Very well, I accept your apology."

I sighed, relief sweeping over my body. "Does that mean you'll come back?"

"Perhaps," Ericka smirked and lifted a brow, "but I have conditions."

I nodded eagerly. "Of course you do."

"But I'll let Finch tell you those." Ericka pulled away from my grasp, and this time, I let her, watching her hips as they swayed toward the door.

When the door closed behind her, I sank back into the bed. That had hurt and not just figuratively. I reached under the blankets Ericka had tucked back around me, and my fingers came back tinged with blood. It was taking longer to heal than usual. No doubt it was because I had used so much of my power. I didn't like to use my family's magic if I didn't have to. It tapped into the very essence of the Spring Court, and while it made me powerful enough to defeat a dragon as grand as Shirazan, it drained me fast and made me unpredictable. I was just lucky no one else got hurt.

That was when Finch appeared in the doorway, a scowl on his face.

"So you lived," he mused dryly. "Congratulations. I don't have to serve under your wretched cousin, Phillipe."

I chuckled and shook my head. "Nobody wants that."

"So," Finch glanced toward the closed door and then back to me, "I take it you two had a talk?"

"Yes, she agreed to come back... sort of." I grimaced.

"Sort of?" Finch furrowed his brows and then smacked me on the arm.

"Hey!" I leaned away from him as pain radiated up my arm. "What was that for?"

"For being a complete fool," Finch snapped, waving his hand in the air. "You almost died for the girl, and all you got out of her was a maybe? You did tell her that you loved her, didn't you? That you would die for her and almost did? Shouldn't that count for something?"

I growled and shifted away from him. "Not in those exact words." Before Finch could smack me again, I added, "But I did apologize, and she accepted. She said she'd come back, but she had terms that she would only tell you."

Finch didn't hit me again. Instead, he stepped back and rubbed a hand over his chin. "She didn't mention any conditions to me but if she's coming back at least that's a start." He clapped his hands together and rubbed them. "Now, what are you going to do to woo her? The gardens are obviously out of the question after the disaster last time. I'm thinking--"

"A dinner," I interrupted him.

"A dinner?" Finch's brows shot up as he flipped his hair over his shoulder. "You can't expect to woo her that way. You need to be extravagant and really put it all out there."

"Not for this woman." I shook my head and threw my legs over the side of the bed. "She isn't impressed with flowers and riches. No, if I'd learned anything about Ericka Burner is that the way to her heart is through food, and you are going to help me."

"Me?" Finch gaped, pointing a finger at his chest. "What can I do? I've never cooked anything in my life and neither have you for that matter."

I shrugged. "It can't be that hard. Besides, I'm sure Jasmine would be happy to help her king impress her friend."

Finch groaned and slapped his face. It wasn't a very encouraging sign, but I would take what I could get.

Chapter 23

Ericka

WE RODE BACK TO the palace in silence. Well, I was silent. Finch was going on and on about all the repairs which would have to be done to the little village and how he would need to get someone out there immediately.

I did feel bad for the brownies. If not for me, they wouldn't have had any of this happen to them. Then again, my eyes slid over to Balefire on the opposite side of the carriage Finch had found for us. If Balefire hadn't frightened me into leaving, then this wouldn't have happened. Then Shirazan would have simply tried to kill me in the castle and not in someone else's home.

I grunted.

Balefire's blazing blue eyes shot from Finch to me. A curious frown covered those lovely lips, and I couldn't bring myself to look away from him. After a moment, he smiled.

My cheeks flaming, I promptly turned back to the scenery outside the carriage. Not for the last time, I wished that Bea had joined us. She would have kept the conversation going without me having to do anything. Though Finch was doing a well enough job with his one-sided conversation. All he needed was the occasional grunt from me or Balefire to keep going.

Cailean and Bea had decided to keep going once the elusive Freddie had returned to fix the carriage. They had deliveries to make, and Bea had a wedding to go to. So, we said our goodbyes and exchanged promises to see each other again. However, now that I was headed back to the palace, I wasn't sure what was going to happen. Was everything going to go back to the way it was? Me in the kitchen and the king... doing whatever the king did?

I wouldn't have long to figure it out in any case. The carriage pulled into the gates of the palace, and servants rushed to help us out of the carriage... or more like help the king. Not that he needed the help, of course. He was a big man, who sometimes had big feathery wings and horns. From what I'd seen, he could clearly take care of himself.

As I stepped out of the carriage from behind Balefire and Finch, there were more than a few eyes on me. No doubt they were curious to know why I was with them, but I wasn't in the mood to explain. Let them wonder.

Neither Finch nor Balefire stopped to explain to me what would happen next, both of them were talking in low voices headed for the palace. I guess that answered my question. For all Balefire's apologies, he had never confirmed or denied what Bea and the others claimed. That he loved me. I guess it was silly to hope that he did. He had saved me after all.

It was probably just his sense of duty as the king that made him do it. That's all.

Tucking my hair behind my ear, I watched my feet as I sighed and made toward the kitchen. Jasmine and the other would want to know I was back. I didn't get five feet before my head banged into the back of someone. Jerking my head up, I automatically began to apologize.

"I'm soo sorry, I wasn't looking where I was going and--" I cut myself off when I realized it was the king who I'd bumped into. Grinning from ear to ear, Balefire placed one hand on his hip and the other tapped his chin.

"Now, where have I heard that excuse before?"

I crossed my arms over my chest and narrowed my eyes at him. "At least this time you didn't get pie in the face."

His grin widening, Balefire nodded. "That is a plus, but I have to say I am quite disappointed. I do love your pie."

My face flushed, and I swallowed thickly at the innuendo in his words. "You...you do?"

"Oh, yes." Balefire nodded, his smile now more of a smirk. "In fact, I love your pie so much that I decided to have a dinner in your honor."

Taken aback by his sudden announcement, I gaped at him. "R... really? Why?"

Balefire turned to my side and wrapped an arm around my shoulders, pulling me in close to the warmth of his body. My mind skittered to dangerous things, things that could only be done in the night, and I missed most of what Balefire was saying.

"Ericka? Do you agree?"

I licked my lips and shook my head, glancing up at him. "Huh? I mean, what? Could you repeat that?"

I expected him to get irritated like he usually did with practically anyone else, but for some reason, his eyes were dark, and the tattoos on his body pulsated next to my face. Startled, I jumped away from his arms and stared at him, ready for his wings and horns to sprout out at any moment. Not that they weren't beautiful, but still, one didn't want to get smacked in the face by them.

And still, Balefire watched me with such an intensity, I feared he might be trying to blow me up with his mind. If that was something he could actually do. Then as suddenly as the emotion came, it was gone. He had that carefree grin on his lips once more and ushered me into the palace.

"As I was saying," Balefire continued, his hand now on the small of my back as he guided us further into the palace. The feel of his palm burned into my skin, and I had to focus harder than I ever had in my life on what he was saying and not what my body was doing in reaction to his physical contact. "I will take care of all the preparations, and you can just relax. You've had a trying few days, and I wouldn't want you too tired to come to the dinner held in your honor."

The skin between my brows pinched together tight as I frowned. "Uh, okay, but you've had just as much a trying few days as I have, Your Majesty."

"Balefire," he corrected me.

I watched him cautiously and then drew out, "Right. Balefire. What I'm trying to say is that you shouldn't have to do so much work either. Let the kitchen staff take care of it. Isn't that what we're here for?"

"See?" Balefire stopped us in the middle of the hallway and pointed a finger at me. "You consider yourself part of the kitchen staff, which means that if I left it to them, you would be right down there helping."

Before I knew what he was doing, he clasped my hands with his and drew me closer. My eyes widened, and they darted around us. Balefire didn't seem to care about the other people in the hallway staring at us, but I did. There were enough rumors around us as it was.

"Please, Ericka. Promise me you won't help with this dinner." The sincerity in his voice was what got me. I couldn't say no to him, not when he was like this. When he was a raging jackass, then sure, I had no problem sticking it to him. Things were much simpler when we both despised the other.

Wait. When did I stop despising him?

Caught up in my own thoughts, Balefire squeezed my hands to get my attention. My eyes snapped back to him as he chuckled.

"Are you sure you're not the one who dropped twenty feet from the sky and not me?"

I smiled slightly. "Honestly, I'm beginning to wonder myself."

"So, can I have your promise?"

Staring up at him for a moment, I cocked my head to the side. "You know a promise from a human doesn't mean much? It's not like we have to tell the truth."

Once again, his reaction surprised me. Instead of threats and yelling, Balefire leaned down until our faces were inches apart and whispered, "Unlike other humans, I trust you, Ericka Burner."

It was high praise from any fae to trust another person, especially a human. I didn't know what to say to it, so instead, I withdrew my hands from his and took a step back.

"I promise." Then before Balefire could confuse me even more, I spun on my heel and darted for my room. I needed a moment alone, to get my head on straight and figure out what exactly in all of Elphame was going on.

Unfortunately, my desire to be alone wasn't meant to be. When I opened the door to my room I was greeted with Finch and Odette, the palace seamstress. Confused, I closed the door behind me and approached them.

"What's going on here?"

Finch turned from Odette and the swaths of fabric in her four arms to give me a sly grin. "The king talked to you, didn't he?"

"Uh, yes. We're having dinner." The sinking feeling in my gut was joined by a sneaky suspicion about what Odette was doing here. "I don't need a new dress for it. I can wear what I have."

"The horror!" Odette gasped, placing all four hands to her chest. "How could you think that those rags could be befitting for dinner with the king? Do you have no sense of decorum?"

I shook my head and stepped closer to them. "It's not like it's a big deal. It's just dinner. It's not a date."

Finch and Odette exchanged a look before looking at me expectantly.

"Wait." I held up a finger and searched the two of them. "It's not a date, right? Because Balefire, the king, said it was a dinner in my honor and said nothing about a date." My breathing quickened as I felt a panic attack coming on.

Finch placed a hand on my arm with a small smile. "The king isn't very good at being completely forthright. Perhaps he thought you might reject the idea."

I shook my head and took a step back. Naturally, my foot caught on the dais Odette had placed in the center of my room, and when I landed on hard on my butt, I winced.

"This doesn't make any sense," I muttered. "My brain feels like it is going to explode."

"Of course it does," Odette sniffed as she lifted up one fabric of a soft rose color and then another of shimmering yellow. "But for us, it's been obvious from the beginning. The king is head over feet for you, you're just too daft to see it." When I opened my mouth to argue, she corrected herself. "Too human."

"How am I too human?" I glared. "I'm around fae all the time, I know how you all are. If I thought for a moment that the actions of the king were declarations of affection, then I would have-"

"You would have what?" Finch asked, shifting my attention toward him from my place on the floor. "Denied him? Run away sooner? You already knew that he had a strange interest in you from the beginning. But, for all the fae you live around, work with, and are friends with, you aren't fae. You don't know what it's like to be a fae in love. We don't act the same way a human would."

I tapped my fingers on my bent knees and thought. Unfortunately, Finch was right. Humans were very straight forward in their affections. The normal thing to do when you liked someone was to be nice to them, maybe even give them a gift, and then invite them out to dinner or a festival.

Fae were quite different. Everything was about keeping the upper hand in their world. No one seemed to want to let the other one know how they felt first. There were games of who could get the other to admit it first and who could trick the other into giving their hand away, games that I had little time or patience for. With a sigh of frustration, I peered up at Finch and Odette.

"What am I supposed to do? He can't want to be with me. I'm the baker and human at that. No one would approve of us."

"So, you do care for him," Finch pointed out, completely off topic, or so I thought.

I narrowed my eyes at him. "I didn't say that. I'm simply stating all the reasons we shouldn't be together. Never did I say I was entertaining the idea of being with the king."

"You are dumber than I thought then," Odette snorted.

My gaze jerked to the seamstress. "Why's that?"

Huffing, she placed her four hands on her hips and stared me down with those golden eyes of hers. "Because all I'm hearing are excuses of why you think you shouldn't be together and no reason why you should be. You, my dear human, are good for him."

"What?" I gaped at her. "You think I'm good for him? He's done nothing but torment me the entire time I've been here."

"Yes, and so he's actually done his job without murdering someone every other week because of his temper," Odette pointed out as if my mental sanity was a small price to pay for peace.

Turning to Finch, I begged him to help me. "Tell me this is crazy. You can't actually believe any of those garbage?"

"It's true." Finch shrugged and grinned, his eyes twinkling with glee. "The king had been more tolerable since you came to the palace, even more so today than before. I haven't once had to talk him out of taking someone's head, because his head is too full of you."

He pointed a finger at me, and I sighed in defeat, burying my head in my lap. I only languished that way for a moment. With a disbelieving shake of my head, I stood up.

"Okay, alright. I will pretend that this makes any sense and go to this dinner of his. A date." I sighed and laughed. "I'd always wanted to go on a date. I guess I never expected my first one to be with the king.”

Finch and Odette laughed with me, then they went about helping me choose a dress for dinner. I had no clue what someone should wear on a date, let alone one with the king. We settled on a soft pink fabric that shimmered in the light. The dress Odette conjured up for me had a full skirt that swayed when I moved. Cinched at the waist, it curved up and over my breasts, leaving my shoulders and arms bare. They then picked out long elbow length gloves which I promptly removed the first moment they turned their backs on me.

After that, Odette had a small man with squinty eyes, a large nose, and a scowl on his face do my hair. His name was Kit, and he was a golem. Not hard to figure out since his skin was the color of wet clay which looked as if it might slip down his face at any moment. I was hesitant to let him touch my hair after I spent so long washing it, but while he might look to be made of clay he didn’t leave bits of himself everywhere he went.

“Wow,” I gasped at my hair after Kit was done, turning this way and that to get a look at the complicated up-do made of braids and beads. “You did a great job!”

Kit stood back his arms over his chest as he nodded in the mirror behind me. “Yeah, it’ll do, but if you are planning any more appearances, I suggest you see me regularly so that I can keep your hair from getting into the mess it was before."

I ignored the dig at my hair and smiled fondly at him. "It means a great deal to me. The king will love it."

With a sniff, Kit sauntered away, leaving me alone in my room for the first time that day. Which, of course, meant that my nerves came back with a vengeance. What in all of Elphame was I getting myself into? Was I really going to go on a date with Balefire?

Sure, he was attractive. He saved my life when he didn't have to, and sometimes he was clever. Funny even.

However, he also was a brute. A tyrant. And a down right bully.

But since he almost died for me, he'd changed. He'd even apologized, something I never thought I'd see come from his mouth. Now, he wanted to honor me with a dinner. I shook my head, carefully not to mess up my hair as I paced back and forth in my room. I told Finch I'd go, but I didn't promise that I would admit any sort of feelings for him. If I had any at all. I mean, he was just so... so irritating!

A soft knock on my door interrupted my tirade. Marching over to it, I swung it open and snapped, "What?"

Luke, the faun, stepped back, his eyes wide.

"Oh, Luke, I thought you were someone else." I stepped out into the hallway and offered him an apologetic smile. "Were you here to get me for dinner?"

Luke cleared his throat and nodded. "Yes, the king has requested that you join him for dinner."

I eyed him for a moment, wondering if I should decline. I still could. Though I would have gotten all dressed up for nothing then. If this was a real date, the king would have come to me, not have a servant do it, but then again, he was the king. Who knew what he was thinking half the time? Kings ran on a different kind of rules for what was proper or not.

I inclined my head and sighed. "Very well. Let's get this over with."

Chapter 24

Balefire

NERVES DANCED ACROSS MY hands and made them shake. I'd done everything I could to prepare for this night. I helped the kitchen make a meal I hoped would impress Ericka. My appearance in the kitchen had been a surprise for sure, but I assured them that I only wished to help.

"Then you have to make sure that the top is golden brown before you pull it from the oven." Jasmine said at my elbow. "See how the top is still a bit white?"

"Yes." I stared with intensity at the top of the pie that was taking an eternity to bake.

"That means that it's not done yet, and a quick tip?" I glanced over to Jasmine who grinned. "Staring at it won't make it get done faster."

"Oh, right." I straightened and moved away from the stove. Glancing around the kitchen, pride swelled in my chest at what we had accomplished. Not only had I prepared my own pie, but I had cut the vegetables and steeped them in a honeysuckle glaze. I'd beat goose meat into perfection, then, under Jasmine's watchful eye, I grilled them over the fire until they were juicy and delicious. The other servants had gone about their own tasks after Jasmine had chastised them for staring. I guess I didn't come down here enough for them to be used to my presence.

I'd have to change that.

Turning to Jasmine as I removed my apron from around my neck, I smiled. "I appreciate you letting me take over the kitchen today. I know it's not something I usually do."

Jasmine placed her hands on her hips and looked over what we'd done. "Well, if you weren't the king, I'd say you'd have a fine future in the culinary arts. As it is, I'm just happy you are doing this for Ericka. She needs a bit of happiness." She turned to the counter and handed off some of the used dishes to the redheaded girl who'd spoken to me before. "She's good for you, you know."

"What?" I gave her a sharp look.

"Ericka." Jasmine smiled softly. "We can all tell. While you started off rough, she's changed you. For the better."

I shifted in place, uncomfortable with her words even as they made my insides sing. "I just hope she feels the same way."

"Humans are different than us, Your Majesty." Jasmine placed a pale blue hand on my arm. "You can't expect them to understand your feelings by your actions alone, especially with how you two started out."

"I know." I frowned and dragged a hand through my hair. It came back covered in flour. Cooking was an adventure I'd never taken part in, but it seemed to be quite a messy one. I turned back to Jasmine. "I hope to change that tonight, but first, I have to get cleaned up. It wouldn't do to show up to dinner like this." I gestured to my flour and food splattered clothing.

Jasmine chuckled along with some of the other ladies. "No, I suppose not." She paused for a moment and then nodded. "You did good. She will be impressed."

"I hope so."

With those final words, I walked toward the kitchen doors. There wasn't much time left before Luke would bring Ericka down. I would have to hurry if I wanted to be to dinner on time. Hurrying to my room, I bypassed Finch who had just stepped out of Ericka's room.

"Is she ready?" I asked hopefully.

"Yes, as ready as she'll ever be." Finch's brows rose as he took a look at my attire. "You, however, could use some work."

I grinned. "I know. I'm late."

"Well, don't let me keep you on my account." Finch waved me off, and I rushed to my room.

His voice stopped me at the door though. "Though I would caution you to be upfront about this dinner when she arrives. She had no idea you thought of this as a date."

I sighed and shook my head. "I've already been told off by Jasmine. I don't need a scolding from you as well."

"I'm just saying--"

I cut him off. "Did I stop being king, and now everyone thinks it's their job to tell me what I'm doing wrong?"

"Since you fell for a common human." Finch snorted and laughed. "No one wants to see that poor girl hurt. Least of all by you."

I frowned, remembering how I'd almost done permanent damage to Ericka. With grief in my heart, I murmured, "I would never hurt her. Not like that, not ever again."

"I know that, but she doesn't." Finch stepped up behind me and patted my back. "That's what this dinner is for. To put the past behind you and start anew. Now, go clean up before she thinks you stood her up."

Huffing, I raced into my room and discarded my clothes so quickly that I was sure I had torn something in two. Then I took the quickest bath of my life, not even waiting for the water to warm. I used the heat of my hand to dry my hair into some semblance of order and then pulled out my very best suit for the occasion: a jacket of pale blue with gold lining and matching buttons, laid over a white shirt and dark blue pants. I pulled my ebony black knee high boots on and stared at myself in the mirror. The clock struck six. I scowled at my reflection. It would have to do.

As I pulled the bedroom door open, I caught sight of Luke standing at Ericka's door his hand poised to knock. Damn, I was late. I rushed out of my room and down the hallway before Ericka could answer the door. I took the stairs three at a time and then jumped the last set, earning me a curious and appalled looks from those left wandering around the palace. I waved them off with a sheepish grin and walked stiffly to the dining room.

Jasmine and her helpers were just putting the final plates out and lighting the candles. When they saw me, the other servants scattered, but Jasmine stayed behind.

"What do you think?" she crossed her arms and looked over the table.

"It looks..." I frowned as I saw the two place settings on the opposite side of the table from one another. "Wrong. All wrong."

"Wrong? How?" she sputtered, searching for what I saw.

Not telling her what it was, I went to the end of the table and picked up Ericka's plate. Walking to the other side, I placed it down next to mine. Realization covered Jasmine's face, and she hurried to move the rest of the place setting to where I'd moved the plate.

"I suppose you can't very well woo her if she's five feet away." Jasmine winked and grinned. Ericka's voice and the distinct sound of footsteps coming closer pulled both of our attention to the doorway. "I'll just be in the kitchen. Good luck!"

Jasmine ducked into the kitchen just as Ericka looking a vision walked through the door, looking like a vision made real. Luke stopped behind her and bowed deeply to me before he too disappeared into the kitchen. Ericka glanced to where Luke disappeared and then back to where I stood. Her mouth fell open, and her eyes widened a fraction as she took in the food and, I hoped, me.

"Wow, Jasmine and the others did a great job." Ericka moved slowly into the room, her fingertips trailing across the table cloth. She took note of the seating arrangement and stopped. "I'll have to thank them after this."

"I already did." I approached her and took her hand in mine before drawing her over to her chair. She allowed me to lead her to her seat and push the chair in. Then, after taking my seat at the head of the table, I shifted in my seat. "Jasmine and the others helped me put this together. I wouldn't have been able to do it without them."

"You... cooked? And you thanked them?" Her mouth fell open slightly and then she caught herself, clamping her mouth shut. "I guess you *are* full of surprises."

Silence fell over the table as we both tried to figure out what to say next. I had planned this dinner, and while I had impressed her, I was at a loss of what to do next. Thankfully, I didn't have to figure it out yet.

Luke and another girl I didn't know came into the dining room. They began serving us from the dishes and filling our cups with pixie wine. I took a long drink of it for the extra boost of confidence, and as I sat my cup down, I turned to Ericka.

"Have I told you have absolutely ravishing you look?"

Ericka flushed and looked down at her plate. "No, you haven't. Odette did a great job."

I placed my hand on hers, and she stiffened. Not letting it dissuade me, I urged her to look up at me.

"No, it's you. Odette might have made the dress, but only you could look the way you do in it. Only you could..." I trailed off as the words caught in my throat.

"Only I could... what?" she prompted me, sliding her hand further into mine. When I didn't answer right away, she squeezed my hand. "I know you're used to getting what you want with a snap of your fingers, but you're going to have to give me a bit more than just saying I look nice."

"I believe I said ravishing, not nice." I held her gaze as she smiled.

"That you did." Releasing my hand, she picked up her fork and tried a piece of the goose.

A low moan came from her lips, making my cock harden immediately. "This is really good."

"I'm glad you think so," I replied as I cut into my own food. "I really wanted to impress you."

"You did?" Her brows lifted, and then her eyes narrowed. "Why?"

I let my lips curl up into a smile. "It's not a secret how I feel about you, Ericka Burner."

She laughed, a sound that made my pulse race and my need to kiss her greaten. "To everyone else it seems but not to me." She gestured to the table with her fork. "You have yet to explain any of this to me." She then settled me with an inquiring stare. "Is this a date?"

I choked on my wine at her question. Coughing, I sat my cup down and turned to her.

"I hadn't called it such, but yes, I had hoped this would be a date. One of many in fact. If... you want to, that is?"

Ericka flushed at the intensity of my gaze, her eyes darting down to her plate. "Well, I don't know, Your Maj-- I mean, Balefire. We haven't exactly been on the best of terms... ever. Why would you even want to date me?"

I was silent for a moment as I thought of the right words. Then I turned to her and took her hands in mine.

"I was wrong to treat you the way I did. I didn't know what my heart was telling me at the time or what Finch was." I laughed. "The bastard knew how I felt about you before I did."

"And how's that? How do you feel about me?"

Shifting my chair closer to her, I reached out and tucked a stray hair over her ear.

"You're smart, witty, and make a damn good pie," I began, starting with the easy things to recount. "You're also a right pain in the ass, but you never play games with me. You say exactly how you feel when you feel it the consequences be damned." I paused as I watched her expression. "It's refreshing to have someone so completely open in a world full of fae who skip around their words and feelings because they want to keep the upper hand. I have never met a woman, fae or human, like you, Ericka Burner."

Ericka was quiet for a long time as her thoughts swirling over her face. When the second part of my surprise came in, a quartet of musicians, her expression changed. A soft melody filled the room, and something changed on Ericka's face. What it was, I couldn't tell.

"Come," she stood and pulled me up by my hand. "Let's dance."

"Dance?"

I stared down at her as she placed her hand on my shoulder and guided my other hand to her waist. I hadn't been this close to her, in such an intimate setting before. I was having a hard time thinking straight. We moved to the music with only a few inches between us. Each of us seemed unsure if we should close the distance. While I had high hopes for this evening, we were moving in the right direction. I just had to make her see how genuine my feelings were. I hadn't been able to say it to myself yet, let alone to her, but I knew what Finch and everyone else in the palace seemed to know.

I loved her.

I loved everything about Ericka Burner. The human who had insulted me at every turn. Put a pie in my face at our first meeting. She had this undeniable fight in her that made me want to keep her close. Not to mention how her eyes lit up when she tasted something delicious or the small sounds she made when something was beyond her taste buds, her words not mine. I wanted to know everything about her. To catch up on what I'd missed because of my own stupidity.

To my surprise, while I was thinking, Ericka had been having her own battle inside of herself. Her battle apparently went somewhere good because she closed the distance between us and placed her head on my chest. My heart skipped a beat. I held my breath as I held her closer.

We danced for a long time before the quartet finally stopped. Ericka pulled back from me, but before she could go back to her seat, I gave her hand a small tug and drew her closer. Leaning down, I searched her face for any sign that she would object before I lowered my face.

As I closed my mouth over hers, it was like I'd been waiting for my whole long life for this moment. She sighed into the kiss, wrapping her arms around my neck as she pulled me closer. I vaguely heard the quartet leaving, but I ignored them, only having eyes for her.

I cupped the back of her neck, sliding my tongue across her lips. Opening up to me, she tentatively touched her tongue with mine. A fire ignited inside of me, and I kissed her deeper, pressing her as close to me as I could and still it wasn't enough.

Ericka responded in kind. Not pushing me away, but tugging on my jacket, sliding her hands beneath it to feel my chest beneath my shirt. I withdrew from her, my eyelids heavy as I stared down at her. Her lips were puffy, and her eyes were hooded. Her desire permeated the air and I sucked in a breath.

My hands clenched at her hips and neck, not sure if she wanted to continue or if I should leave it at that. Ericka had her own ideas.

A glance back at the dinner, she then smiled up at me, a seductive smile that I'd never thought in a million years I'd see on her face. She took one of my hands and led me out of the dining room. We exchanged secretive looks and once stopped in an alcove to kiss again. By the time we made it to my bedroom, neither of us could wait any longer.

Clothes were discarded and hands roamed. Her skin was softer than I ever imagined. Her taste just as sweet as the pixie wine we'd drank at dinner. As I lowered her to the bed, I feared I wouldn't last long once I was inside of her.

"You drive me crazy," I murmured to her as I took in her nude form. "I never knew someone could fill my mind so completely until you."

Ericka giggled and stroked the side of my face. "I'll take that as a compliment."

I pressed another kiss to her lips, before trailing my mouth down her neck. Cupping her breasts in my hands, she arched her back for me. I suckled on the tip of each of them, enjoying the way she moaned and pulled at me to get closer.

My fingers trailed down her thighs, lifting and separating them. The scent of her filled my senses and it took everything in me not to shove myself inside of her now.

"Have you ever?" I blinked through my need, my cock brushing against her entrance.

Shaking her head, Ericka breathed, "No. I haven't."

"I'll be careful," I reassured her, taking her mouth with my own once more. My hand snaked between us as I stroked the apex of her thighs. She gasped into my mouth at the same time I slid inside.

The feel of her clenching around me, made my breath still. I wasn't going to last long. A glance at her face, her eyes squeezed shut but not in pain but pleasure, reassured me it was okay to move. Trying to make sure she felt as much pleasure from the act as I did, I circled her sensitive bud as I thrust my hips. Each gasp and cry of want from her lips, spurred me on and soon we were both falling over the edge.

Afterwards, she curled around my side as I stroked her back. Her breathing evened and I soon fell asleep to the side of her breath.

Light filtered into the bedroom. I blinked against the stinging rays and shifted on the bed. A groan came from my bed partner and I froze. I had almost forgotten. I didn't know how, I could still feel what it was like to be inside of her. What Ericka sounded like as she orgasmed.

I smiled down at Ericka, who slept with her mouth open and her body sprawled out across the bed. The dinner had been everything and more than I'd hoped for. I certainly didn't regret what happened. I hoped she didn't either.

I frowned. While she had pulled all manner of confessions from me last night, not once had she told me how she felt. It should have made me feel vulnerable. The same way I would feel with another fae who held all the cards, but with Ericka, it only made me want to prove to her how much I loved her even more.

Standing slowly from the bed so as not to wake her, I pulled my discarded clothes back on. I jotted a noted down on a piece of paper so she wouldn't wonder where I went before rounding the bed.

Glancing down at her one last time, I stroked my hand over her hair, leaning down to kiss her forehead. With that handled, I placed the note on the bedside table and headed for the door. Breakfast in bed coming up.

Chapter 25

Ericka

AS WAKEFULNESS INCHED FORWARD, I snuggled further into the blankets. Blankets that were far softer than the ones I remembered. Then last night jumped to my mind.

My eyes flew open and I sat up. The covers fell, revealing my bare chest to the room. As I hurriedly clutched the blankets to my chest, my eyes dropped to the empty spot beside me.

Balefire was gone.

Part of me was relieved because it gave me a moment to put my mind back together. The other part was a bit disappointed. Why had he left without waking me?

I threw the blanket off, causing a breeze that sent several of the papers on his nightstand to fly onto the floor. Ignoring the papers, I searched for my clothes. As I pulled last night's dress back on, I tried to figure out what I was going to do.

What had I been thinking last night? One nice dinner and I'd hopped right into bed with him?

Sure, he'd confessed his feelings for me, but I never figured I would have done something like that. Still, last night was just so perfect, and he was so perfect.

He was nothing like the brute he'd shown me from before. Then again, he hadn't been that way for a few days now. It made me feel slightly better about myself, but confusion and doubt still filled my mind.

Going to the bedroom door, I pulled it out and peaked my head out. No one was in the hallway, so I hustled over to my bedroom door. Jumping inside just as a set of footsteps came down the hallway, I leaned back against the door and let out a long breath.

I searched my wardrobe for something else to wear and exchanged it for the gown. My thoughts and feelings swirled like a tornado in me, and nausea pushed forward at the combination.

Okay, I just needed to think.

I sat on the edge of my bed and held my head in my hands as thoughts of last night rolled in my mind. Everything had been wonderful. Balefire had gone above and beyond to make me something for our dinner date. He had made something for me. I laughed. Who would have thought the king would get his hands dirty for a lowly human? Certainly not me. Then again no one would think he would kill his favorite pet dragon for me either.

I sighed and let myself sink off the edge of the bed and onto the floor as I covered my face with one hand. Everything was so complicated and discombobulated. I couldn't figure out up from down let alone how I felt right now.

The dinner had been great. Wonderful. Fabulous. Any manner of word right now would describe it, except bad. Then there was the wine and the music. I felt so content, while somewhat still a bit awkward, but it had more to do with the date itself than Balefire. I was used to being alone with him. He made me nervous for different reasons.

Sometimes those reasons weren't good ones, especially when he was being a right ass. Other times though... I shivered at the memory of his arms around me as we danced, how his heartbeat raced when I placed my head on his chest. It was obvious that he hadn't bent the truth with me. In fact, he'd been so blatant about everything it would be hard to find a lie in it all.

The only thing he hadn't said to me last night was that he loved me.

Could you blame him? You didn't exactly tell him how you felt either. You let him do all the talking and then jumped him like a siren in heat.

Okay, so yes, I hadn't really put my own cards on the table, but he was the king, and up until a week or so ago, he hadn't exactly been the nicest to me. It was a bit hard to trust this new him.

But I wanted to.

I wanted to trust him. To let him love me. To love him.

Oh, if my parents could see me now. I giggled to myself, leaning my head back against the side of my bed. No one back home would believe that I not only had the love of the king but that I'd bedded him.

Which brought me back to the matter that he had been gone when I woke up. If he cared for me like he said he did, then why didn't he leave a note? Or even tell me where he was going before leaving like that? I wanted to believe that it was for a good reason, but the warnings I'd gotten before about fae men getting bored once they caught you came rushing forward.

Had that been it? Was he done with me now that he had me? But the things he said last night couldn't have been lies. Fae didn't lie. Ever.

I rubbed my chest where my heart hurt. I didn't know what to do now. Did I go back to the room or act like nothing happened and go back to work? I still hadn't had a chance to talk to Jasmine and the others. Though, I was sure based on last night's dinner they knew I was back.

Sighing, I stood and put my shoes on. I guess I would just wait and see how Balefire acted. All I could do now was to go back to work and hope things were going to be different. Besides, my mind was too confused to do anything but shove my hands into some dough right now.

An hour later and I was elbow deep in the sink as I washed some of the dishes that I needed for what I was going to make. Jasmine had welcomed me back with open arms and a sly grin that I wished she'd put away. The other had giggled and tiptoed around me like I was some kind of unicorn.

"So..." Sybil cozied up beside me. "How was your date with the king?"

I huffed a laugh, wiping my hands off on a towel. "Does everyone know?"

The collection of giggles in the room answered my question. Shaking my head, I turned to the counter and gathered my supplies. I needed to keep busy, or my brain was going to explode.

"Last night was..." I trailed off, knowing the whole room was listening. "Nice."

"Nice?" Sybil screeched, jumping up and down with glee. "You spent the night with the king, and it was just fine?"

I flushed and didn't bother asking how they knew, my hands busy pouring and stirring. "Uh, I guess it was a bit better than fine."

"I would hope so."

My eyes jerked up to the grinning face of the devil himself. My heart ratcheted up a notch and my hand stirred the bowl in my hand even faster.

"Uh, hi." I peeked up at him and then back to my bowl.

Balefire stepped closer to the table, and the kitchen went silent at his appearance. His hands appeared before me on the other side of the table. I glanced up at him as he leaned forward.

"You weren't in the bedroom when I came back," he said as his voice dipped low.

I lifted the now-ready dough out of the bowl and placed it on the flour covered counter before me. "Neither were you."

Balefire frowned, his brows furrowing together. His confusion might have been cute had we not had so much unresolved tension between us, besides the fact that we had an audience.

"Didn't you get my note?"

I kneaded the dough harder, jerking my head up to meet his gaze. "What note?"

Balefire shifted, his eyes darting to the onlookers who were not being discreet at all. Then his eyes locked back onto me, those gorgeous, soul-searching eyes that had my body quaking with remembrance of last night. "The note I left you by the bed."

Now it was my turn to be confused. Then I remembered the papers that had scattered across the floor in my haste to get out of there. The note from him must have been in that. Oops.

Trying to save face, I shrugged. "I didn't see a note."

"Hmm." Balefire hummed and then reached across the counter. My hands stopped what they were doing when his larger one sat on top of mine. "Can we go somewhere more private? To talk?"

Staring up at him for a moment, I glanced around the room for something I could use to distract me from this conversation but no one was going to help me out. Guess, I should just get it over with. With a sigh, I lifted my hands and wiped them off on my apron, then took my apron off and sat it on the counter. I turned to Jasmine.

"Could you finish this for me? I'll be right back."

Jasmine nodded, her eyes darting from me to Balefire. "Of course."

Rounding the counter, I allowed Balefire to place his hand on my lower back and lead me out of the kitchen. We didn't stop in the dining room but he kept walking. Confused at where we were going but not ready to be the first person to start the conversation, I let him take me down a hallway and toward the east side of the castle. When we stopped before a pair of familiar glass paned doors, I screeched to a stop, digging my heels in and shaking my head.

"What's wrong?" Balefire dropped his hand and turned to me.

"Last time I went in there you almost fed me to Shirazan. I might be slow but I'm not about to repeat my mistakes." I took a step backward, my eyes on the door.

"I'm sorry if I scared you, Ericka. I never meant for it to go that far." Balefire's expression darkened and shame crossed his face. "The garden is a touchy subject for me, one that I hope to one day share with you. But for now," he took the few steps to close the distance between us and placed his hands on my shoulders, "I want to show it to you. If you let me."

Still nervous but not so fearful to decline him, I jerked my head up and down once. "Alright."

With Balefire's arm around my waist and my throat thick with worry, he pushed the door open and led me inside.

The garden was just as beautiful as it had been the first time I'd come with Sybil. The trees glistened in the morning light, their leaves fragile yet strong. Flowers covered every inch of the plush green ground we walked on as we made our way down the path. I knew where he was taking us without knowing. I'd gone there myself out of some kind of strange instinct, like the rose wanted me to come.

The sight of the rose locked in its metal and glass cage made my chest ache. This was where he had taken me. Where he had gotten so angry with me. Before everything between us seemed like some kind of game of who could push the other farthest. It wasn't until the day he found me in the gardens that he had really showed how beastly he could be.

"Ericka," Balefire whispered in my ear, "it's alright. I never want to scare you like that ever again. Actually, I make a promise right here and now, to always hold my temper and think before I act."

"That's a big promise." I told him, glancing from the rose to him. "You're fae your promises are binding are you sure you can live up to it?" I laughed nervously, trying to break the tension.

"For you?" Balefire cupped the sides of my face and leaned forward until our breath mingled. "I could do anything."

My heart jerked in my chest at his words and I couldn't help but smile. "Anything? Really?"

Chuckling at my sass, Balefire kissed me softly and then murmured, "I love you, Ericka Burner. I think I've loved you from the moment you threw a pie in my face."

"I did not throw a pie in your face," I scoffed. "I tripped. You just happened to be in the way."

Balefire threw his head back and laughed. "Still, I couldn't imagine what could have become of me had I picked one of the other bakers over you."

I smirked. "You'd probably have died of food poisoning by now."

Shaking his head as he held me closer. "See? I couldn't live without that smart mouth of yours. But what I really want to know... is could you?"

My mouth dried at his question. I was worried he was going to ask something like this. I hadn't fully grasped all my feelings for the fae before me just yet. There was a mixture of emotions in me from the first day we met, when I thought he was Angus and not the king up until now after we had come to know each other's bodies and the fae before me became more than the tyrant king set on making me break.

"I..." I started and then paused to catch my breath and give myself courage. "I can't say I love you."

Balefire frowned and stepped back from me, dropping his hands. I quickly kept going, closing the distance between us once more.

"Not without saying something else first." I paused and locked eyes with him. "I forgive you for what you did, and I also know that for me to love you, I have to love every part of you. While you are fae, there are things about being human that require more."

"More?"

"Yes." I nodded, urged on by his willingness to listen. "I don't want to play power games with you. Flexing your latest conquest to me won't make me want to be with you. Being there for me, listening to me," I glanced around the garden and smiled, "sharing parts of you with me. That's what will make this work."

"So... you're saying you love me?" Balefire smirked, jumping right into it before I could even get the words out.

I laughed and shook my head. "I'm saying that I have feelings for you. Complicated ones that might be love, okay so they probably are but you still have a lot to make up for and I'm not quite done making you pay yet."

"I thought you didn't want to play games." Balefire frowned

I looked up to the ceiling where the sky beamed through and lifted a shoulder. "Okay, maybe a few games but only when they benefit me."

I screeched as Balefire scooped me up into his arms and then covered my mouth with his own. I kissed him back wholeheartedly, not sure what the future would bring us but more than happy to find out.

When I pulled my mouth away from him, I asked, "What did your note say?"

Grinning down at me, Balefire said, "It said get your ass out of bed and love me."

"It did not!" I giggled and smacked him on the arm. Wrapping my arms around his neck, I brushed my lips over his as I murmured, "I already did."

About the Author

Erin Bedford is an otaku, recovering coffee addict, and Legend of Zelda fanatic. Her brain is so full of stories that need to be told that she must get them out or explode into a million screaming chibis. Obsessed with fairy tales and bad boys, she hasn't found a story she can't twist to match her deviant mind full of innuendos, snarky humor, and dream guys.

On the outside, she's a work from home mom and bookbinger. One the inside, she's a thirteen-year-old boy screaming to get out and tell you the pervy joke they found online. As an ex-computer programmer, she dreams of one day combining her love for writing and college credits to make the ultimate video game!

Until then, when she's not writing, Erin is devouring as many books as possible on her quest to have the biggest book gut of all time. She's written over thirty books, ranging from paranormal romance, urban fantasy, and even scifi romance.
Also, third person is really weird when writing about yourself. Just putting that out there.

Come chat her up!
www.erinbedford.com
Facebook.com/erinrbedford
twitter.com/erin_bedford
Don't forget to follow Erin on Goodreads, Pinterest, Instagram, and YouTube!

Want to be the first to know about Erin's new releases?
Erinbedford.com/newsletter